"You come from a rich family," Melody began.

"I'm from a small town in Georgia and grew up poor. What do I know about the life of a multimillionaire?"

"Maybe you should find out," he said. "People are people. How can you make a judgment without getting to know me?"

"Tonight was wonderful, but this has to be it." Melody wished he would listen to reason, but his mentioning her judgment went right to her guilt. Was she too critical? But this wasn't all about his money. She couldn't forget his love of skydiving and car races—dangerous activities that took lives. She couldn't be with a man who took such risks.

"I won't take no for an answer."

"Please don't make this difficult. It's not just because you come from wealth and I don't. You like to live on the edge, and I like to play it safe. How can that be a good combination?"

He smiled. "It might be fun to find out."

"You don't give up, do you?"

"Not when I want something." Hudson's look could cut steel. "You haven't heard the last of me, Ms. Hammond."

Merrillee Whren is the winner of the 2003 Golden Heart® Award presented by Romance Writers of America. She has also been the recipient of the RT Reviewers' Choice Best Book Award and the MAGGIE® Award for Excellence. She is married to her own personal hero, her husband of thirty-five-plus years, and has two grown daughters. Please visit her website at merrilleewhren.com or connect with her on Facebook at facebook.com/merrilleewhren.author.

Books by Merrillee Whren

Love Inspired

Village of Hope

Second Chance Reunion
Nursing the Soldier's Heart
Falling for the Millionaire

Kellerville

Hometown Promise
Hometown Proposal
Hometown Dad

The Heart's Homecoming
An Unexpected Blessing
Love Walked In
The Heart's Forgiveness
Four Little Blessings
Mommy's Hometown Hero
Homecoming Blessings

Visit the Author Profile page at Harlequin.com for more titles.

Falling for
the Millionaire

Merrillee Whren

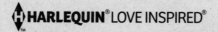

Hᵀᴹ **HARLEQUIN**® LOVE INSPIRED®

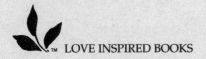 LOVE INSPIRED BOOKS

Recycling programs
for this product may
not exist in your area.

ISBN-13: 978-0-373-71949-5

Falling for the Millionaire

Copyright © 2016 by Merrillee Whren

www.Harlequin.com

Printed in U.S.A.

There is no fear in love. But perfect love drives out fear, because fear has to do with punishment. The one who fears is not made perfect in love.
—*1 John* 4:18

I would like to dedicate this book to my agent,
Pattie Steele Perkins, who helped in
so many ways to make this book a reality.

Chapter One

Blind dates mimicked test-driving cars. Tonight Melody Hammond had another one to deal with. What would it bring? Her friends kept sending her fancy sports cars when all she wanted was a nice simple sedan.

The doorbell rang. She peered through the peephole in the front door of her small brick ranch house in her suburban Atlanta neighborhood. She couldn't tell much from the distorted image except that the man was tall and had dark hair.

This was one date that carried some consequences. Tonight's fund-raiser for The Village of Hope Ministries was an event intended to raise money for Melody's pet project—building more housing for abused and troubled women. Too often the ministry had difficulty finding space for all the women who needed help and had to turn many away. She planned to do everything within her power to see this project funded.

People had paid a lot of money to attend this formal dinner dance, including her date. She hoped it would go well, so she could represent The Village properly. She wanted to believe anyone who had an interest in helping a charity was a decent person. Unfortunately, she'd learned over the years that not all donors to good causes were good people. Some had ulterior motives.

Melody took a deep breath, then tried to produce a genuine smile as she opened the door. That breath caught in her throat as she stared up at Hudson Paine Conrick, the Fourth. In his black tuxedo he was handsome beyond description. His dark hair curled and waved in a rumpled kind of way. The five-o'clock shadow he sported gave him a dangerous look—at least where a woman's heart was concerned.

A Ferrari.

No doubt.

He gave her a lazy grin. "Ms. Hammond, Hudson Conrick. Nice to meet you."

Melody nodded, hoping her brain would engage her tongue. "Please come in while I get my wrap, Mr. Conrick."

"Certainly. You look lovely, though it's a shame you have to cover that stunning red evening gown with anything." He stepped across the threshold.

"Thank you, but a pashmina doesn't cover much. Thankfully, it's not too cold tonight." Smiling, Melody tried not to assign any connotation to his compliment as she grabbed her purse and wrap from the nearby hall table.

"Fortunately, Atlanta is having a mild January." Hudson opened the door for her.

"Thanks." She threw the wrap around her shoulders, then locked the door. Turning toward the driveway, she stopped short at the sight of a black limousine. She caught herself before she blurted, *Wow! A limo!* Was he trying to show off? She shouldn't question their mode of transportation, just enjoy it.

As they approached the vehicle, the driver appeared out of nowhere and opened the door. Melody slid across the black-and-gray leather seats, a combination of butter and silk beneath her fingers. The smell of cleaner permeated the warm interior. A television in one corner broadcasted business news while soft music played in the background. A lit workstation with a laptop computer and a bar filled with rows of glasses sat across from her.

Melody pressed her lips together to keep her mouth from hanging open at the obvious display of wealth. Who was entitled to this much luxury when people were starving?

She had to stop her judgmental attitude. This man was donating a lot of money to her cause. She had no right to disparage his wealth.

As Hudson slid in beside her, he turned off the TV. "Sorry about that. I'm sure you don't want business news blaring at you."

Melody shrugged and let her pashmina fall from her shoulders. "No problem, Mr. Conrick."

Smiling, he reached for a glass from the bar, filled it with ice and poured water into it. "Would you like one? Or a soft drink?"

"Water's fine, thanks."

He poured another glass of water, then handed it to her. "Shall we toast to a wonderful evening?"

"Sure." She clinked her glass against his and wondered what she should talk about now. Hudson settled back and looked at her, his eyes, the color of maple syrup, filled with amusement. "Let's set aside the formality. Please call me Hudson. May I call you Melody?"

The tension in Melody's shoulders began to wither away. "That would make for a better evening."

"Agreed." Hudson grinned. "So you and Ian work together?"

Nodding, Melody wondered whether Ian Montgomery, her co-worker who had set up this date, had any idea how mismatched she and Hudson were. "Yes. In addition to being The Village's legal guy, he's the administrator of the nursing facility and senior center."

Surprise registered on Hudson's face. "That's interesting. I knew he handled your legal stuff, but I didn't know about the rest."

"All of us in the administration at The Village have multiple roles. I came there to head up the women's ministries, but I also coordinate the children's one, too."

"Must keep you busy."

"It does." Melody searched her mind for something to talk about that didn't sound like a commercial for The Village. "Ian said you went to law school with him. Where do you practice law?"

Hudson gave her a lopsided grin. "I don't."

"Oh." Did she dare ask him what he did? Maybe he was one of those trust-fund babies who did little work and spent time vacationing in trendy locations. Ian had mentioned that Hudson had been overseas.

He chuckled. "I suppose you're wondering what I do with my time?"

As a heated blush crept up Melody's neck and onto her cheeks, she was thankful for the dim lighting in the limo. She might as well be honest. "Yes, I'm curious since you don't practice law."

A smirk curved his lips for a moment. "I went to law school because my father insisted on it. Otherwise, he would've cut me off without any money, and I couldn't have that, now, could I? Without that money, I wouldn't have been able to be your escort tonight."

Was he joking, or was he serious? She resisted the urge to rub away the headache that was forming at her temples. How would she endure a whole night with a guy whose only thought was living off his daddy's money? She had to be thankful for that money. It was helping to fund this much-needed project.

Melody forced a smile. "That still doesn't tell me what you do."

"I try my best to stay out of my father's hair." Hudson gave her a sardonic smile.

Another cryptic answer. Maybe he really didn't do anything, and he didn't want to admit it. Sounded as if he didn't get along with his father. Sad. Hudson had a father he didn't have much use for, and Melody wished her father was still alive. He'd died too young in an airplane crash. "That's your job? Staying out of your father's hair?"

Laying his head back, Hudson laughed out loud. When he finally looked at her, his eyes still sparked with laughter. "That's a good description of what I do."

"And how does one accomplish that?"

"Excellent question." Hudson jiggled the ice cubes in his glass as if he would find an answer there. "I work wherever he sends me. I've spent the last year in the Middle East looking out for our oil interests. I've only been back in the States for a few weeks. My mother insisted that I come home for Christmas."

Melody's stomach roiled at the mention of that region of the world. So much trouble. So much misery. So many deaths. "I'm sure your mother was happy."

Hudson nodded as he smiled wryly. "Yes, and I managed to stay on my father's good side for all of Christmas Day. You might as well know that my presence at your fund-raiser tonight is all about pleasing him."

There it was—the ulterior motive. Pleasing his daddy. As reasons went, that one wasn't all bad. At least Hudson was honest about why he was her escort. She realized she was judging the man again. Maybe his daddy was a real reprobate and staying out of his way was a matter of wisdom. She stared at her glass of ice water. Why couldn't she put her critical attitude on ice? "I'm glad you could join us this evening."

"Me, too. It's been a while since I've had the pleasure of going out with a beautiful woman." Hudson's gaze didn't waver as he looked at her.

Melody produced another smile that she feared came across as pretentious as his flattery. How did she acknowledge it? Believe he was sincere? "Thank you for sharing your evening with me and contributing to this very worthy cause."

He set his glass in the cup holder. "Tell me more about The Village of Hope."

"Sure." Melody took a deep breath, wondering whether a wealthy man could begin to understand what it was like to be poor or down on your luck and without resources. "It's a multifaceted ministry. We provide shelter for women who have fled an abusive situation or women who need a helping hand while they recover from addictions. As you know, we provide legal help for those who can't afford it. We have a dozen children's homes for abused, neglected or orphaned children. The Village has a nursing facility and an assisted living center. We also have job counseling and job training."

"Amazing. I had no idea The Village had so many programs. My father only told me about the women's ministry." Hudson laced his fingers behind his head. "Do you have a rehab center?"

Melody shook her head. "We help folks after they've been through rehab to get back on track with their lives. Many facilities send their clients to us after they've completed their program."

"Looks as though we're at the hotel." Hudson slid toward the door.

"The dinner's in the main ballroom." Melody wrapped the pashmina around her shoulders.

After the limo stopped, a doorman immediately opened the door. Hudson stepped out and extended his hand to her. "Ready for a wonderful evening?"

Her heart racing, she placed her hand in his as he helped her out. The callouses on his palm surprised her. She had expected to feel no signs of physical work. "I'm looking forward to it."

Hudson tipped the doorman, and Melody guessed from the expression on the doorman's face that the tip had been very generous. As they entered the lobby, he smiled down at her. That and the warmth of his hand sent a little shiver up her arm and down her spine. Attraction. Should she be feeling it? A sedan, not a sports car. That was what she wanted, but maybe she should enjoy the sports car just for tonight.

While they walked through the lobby toward the ballroom, Hudson slipped her arm through his. For a moment, Melody felt like a princess on the arm of her prince. People turned to look at them. She glanced up at him. *Gorgeous* didn't begin to describe the man. No wonder people stopped to stare. He seemed oblivious to their interest. Did he expect the attention, or was he really a down-to-earth, modest guy?

There was a lot to learn about Hudson Paine Conrick, the Fourth. So far she'd only scratched the surface. Did she want to know him better? What did it matter? After tonight his obligation would be over, and she would probably never see him again. Their circles didn't intersect.

Surveying the area, Melody hoped to see someone from The Village, but few people had arrived yet. As the chandeliers sparkled overhead, she wished Ian and his wife, Annie, could be at their table to help with the date Ian had arranged for her, but folks who worked at The Village would be scattered throughout the ballroom in order to talk to the donors.

Melody glanced at her ticket. "We're at table four."

Hudson raised his eyebrows. "I thought a very important person like you would be at table one."

"We're right in front of the speakers. So we're at a VIP table." Melody waved a hand toward the front.

As she made her way across the ballroom, she stopped to introduce Hudson to folks she knew from area churches. With great ease, he engaged them in conversation. He seemed to know someone or something that related to every person he spoke to. He should be the fund-raiser instead of her.

After they found their seats, Melody set her wrap on her chair. "I hope you don't mind if I leave you here while I check on a few things."

"Trying to get rid of me already?" He grinned as he pulled out his chair.

"No. I wouldn't want to miss another ride in that limo."

He chuckled as he waved her away. "Do what you

have to do. I know this evening is more business than pleasure for you."

"Thanks. I won't be long." Striding toward the doors at the back of the room without a backward glance, she hoped his jovial manner meant he was teasing. Despite their congenial conversation on the ride over and his seemingly pragmatic attitude, being with him put her nerves on edge. She didn't want to do anything to alienate the man. Although the folks in attendance tonight had already made a substantial donation, the object of the event was to convince many of them to make their support ongoing.

Melody hated fund-raising—begging people for money. She struggled with that part of working for a nonprofit entity. Doing cartwheels across the ballroom might be easier. A smile and a prayer would get her through the evening.

Hudson had never met a woman who could walk in heels and an evening gown as fast as Melody. She'd raced away as if some evil force was chasing her. Despite her statement to the contrary, maybe she really was trying to get away from him.

What was it about her that had him second-guessing himself? He usually had to fight women off, although most of them were only interested in his money and the status a relationship with his family would bring. During college, he'd fallen hard for one of those women. Nicole Griffin had fooled him into thinking she loved him, but she'd only wanted to marry a man with influence and wealth. Thanks to his sister Elizabeth, he'd found out before he'd made a big mistake and married Nicole.

Sometimes he wished he could be anonymous. He

wanted to be liked for himself and not his connection to the Conrick millions.

Hudson had promised himself that his presence here tonight would end the bowing and scraping to his father's wishes. He wanted to prove to his dad that he could be his own man and not have to depend on the family business. How could he make his father understand? He could thank his money and Ian for one thing. Melody Hammond. When he'd knocked on her door and found a beautiful woman on the other side, his resentment over having to attend this fund-raiser had dissolved.

Although Melody was with him tonight because of the donation his family had made to The Village, she didn't hang on him or try to impress him like so many women did. There was something different about her—something he couldn't decipher at the moment, but it was something he liked.

Her less-than-genuine smiles puzzled him. He could always look on the positive side of things and believe she was merely nervous about the success of this event. From what his father had told him, lots of dignitaries and movers and shakers were here. He'd been to plenty of these types of functions—most of them boring. But he was looking forward to his evening with Melody.

The sight of her in that red evening gown, with a skirt that swished and flowed around her like the cape at a bullfight, had set his heart racing. The color accentuated her blond hair swept away from her face in a fancy hairdo, set off with some kind of sparkly stuff that matched her dangly earrings. She reminded him of the storybook princesses his nieces were so fond of. As far as blind dates went, she was a ten.

"Look what the cat dragged in." Ian's voice shook Hudson from his musings.

Hudson stood and shook his friend's outstretched hand. "Good to see you. It's been a long time."

Ian glanced around. "Where's Melody?"

"She went to check on something and should be right back." Hudson looked at the petite dark-haired beauty standing next to Ian. "Who is this lovely lady?"

"My wife, Annie." Ian smiled as he looked lovingly at her. "Annie, I'd like you to meet Hudson Conrick."

"Nice to meet you, Hudson. Are you associated with Conrick Industries? I did some consulting with one of their companies years ago."

Nodding, Hudson shook Annie's hand. He couldn't even meet an old friend without his family connections being brought into the conversation. "Yes, my great-grandfather started Conrick Industries in the early 1900s."

Before anyone could make another comment, Melody returned. "Ian, Annie. I'm glad you're here. Where are you sitting?"

"Table three." Annie pointed to the table next to them.

"Oh, good. We're right here." Melody placed a hand on the back of her chair. "We'll be able to talk after the formalities are over."

Hudson took in the relief on Melody's face. Was she merely happy to have her friends nearby, or was she uncomfortable with him? The woman was a riddle—confident and self-assured, yet vulnerable.

"I see my parents." Annie looped her arm through Ian's. "We'd better say hi to them. Talk to you later."

As they walked away, Hudson looked over at Melody. "Ian and I haven't been in touch much since we left law school. I thought I remembered him getting a divorce. Is Annie his second wife?"

Melody stared up at him with her light brown eyes flecked with green. She looked as though she didn't know how to answer. "I'm not sure what to say about that. It's complicated. Maybe you should ask him rather than me."

Shaking his head, Hudson let out a halfhearted laugh. "Did I step into a minefield with that question?"

Melody's face turned ashen, and she took a deep breath as she placed a hand over her heart. "Sorry."

"Don't be sorry." Hudson motioned toward their seat. "Let's sit down and forget I made the inquiry."

Melody nodded, the color still not returning to her cheeks. He pulled out her chair, and she sat down without saying a thing. As he took his seat, Hudson tried to figure out why the discussion had triggered Melody's reaction. Had she and Ian been involved before he married Annie? While Hudson stewed over Melody's reaction, two middle-aged couples approached their table. Melody got up and hugged them all.

Hudson stood as she turned to him and introduced him to Ian's parents, Doreen and Jordan Montgomery, and to Adam Bailey, the administrator of The Village, and his date, Debra McCoy. After the two couples left, Melody greeted the folks who would share their table, an advertising executive and his wife, a couple who owned a printing business and a couple who were both doctors.

The laughter and conversation that buzzed through the ballroom came to an end as Adam Bailey greeted everyone from the podium at the head table. After Adam's greeting, Jordan Montgomery gave a blessing for the event. Immediately following the prayer, the waiters and waitresses served the food.

The discussion during the meal centered on the ministries of The Village. Hudson admired the way Melody maneuvered their talk toward supporting The Village without being pushy. Thankful that she controlled the conversation, he sat back and watched. He didn't have to say a thing, and he appreciated that. Best of all, no one asked him about his family connections. That made for a perfect dinner.

While the servers removed the plates and brought out the desserts, Adam Bailey came to the podium once again and gave a quick talk about The Village. Jordan Montgomery followed with a short but motivational speech that encouraged people to look beyond themselves and help those in need. Soon after, they began the auction of donated items, as well as the silent auction that would be going on during the evening.

The auctioneer entertained the crowd as he moved each article along. Hudson watched Melody's joyous reaction as a quilt made by Lovie Trimble, the receptionist at The Village, garnered five thousand dollars.

When the auction concluded, Adam came back to the podium. He thanked everyone for their participation, then turned and picked up something from a nearby chair. "Ladies and gentlemen, I'd like to honor someone tonight who deserves a lot of credit for this evening's activities. She's the dynamic force behind this project. Please give a huge round of applause for Melody Hammond." Adam looked down at their table. "Melody, come on up here."

The surprise on Melody's face as she stood made Hudson smile. He'd learned from the discussion tonight that her whole life revolved around the women's and children's ministries at The Village. She obviously deserved this award. While she made her way to the stage, the applause grew louder.

Adam gave her a hug and handed her a plaque when she reached the podium. "Considering all the work you do, this isn't much, but we wanted you to know we appreciate everything you've done for The Village."

Taking the plaque, she wiped a tear from her cheek as she faced the audience. "This is certainly a surprise. I want to thank everyone who came out tonight. Thank you for your support of this very important project. You're helping women and children have a better life. I want to especially thank my coworker, Annie Montgomery. Thanks again."

People stood and more applause filled the ballroom as Melody made her way back to the table. Hudson resisted the urge to give her a hug. He didn't know how she would take it. Despite her giving nature in regard to The Village, she seemed personally guarded. He wanted to find out why.

After Melody resumed her seat, Adam announced the dance portion of the evening. When two of the couples from their table went to the dance floor, Ian and Annie came over, sat down and congratulated Melody on her award.

Melody picked up the plaque and looked at Annie. "Did you know about this?"

Annie shook her head. "Adam said he wanted to do something for you, but he never said what."

Melody put the plaque back on the table. "It wasn't necessary."

"Yeah, but it's always nice to get some recognition." Ian nodded his head. "The auction went very well. It brought in a lot of funds."

"I wish Lovie could've been here to see her quilt produce so much money." Melody rubbed a hand across the shiny face of her plaque. "She's attending a grandchild's birthday tonight."

Hudson took in the discussion, his admiration for Melody growing. She'd rather have recognition for a co-worker than for herself. He'd been hanging around the wrong kind of women.

"So what are you doing with yourself these days?" Ian looked at Hudson.

"Not much." Hudson shook his head.

"You could join us at The Village. We could use another attorney now that our financial situation has improved."

"Ian, I've never used that law degree. I wouldn't be of much help." Hudson wished he had a better plan for his life, but he wasn't interested in being a lawyer or a corporate executive. He wasn't sure where he belonged, but he wanted an adventure of his own, not one his father had planned for him. "When the weather gets warmer, I intend to do some skydiving instructions with an outfit near here that does tandem jumps. Anyone want to give it a try?"

Melody's look slipped from astonishment to fear. "You skydive?"

Hudson nodded. "I was a paratrooper in the army. Since I left the service, I've become a certified skydiving instructor. I missed doing that when I was working overseas, so I aim to get back into it. And I have plans to do some race-car driving."

"Wow! Impressive, but I'm not sure I'm that brave." Annie chuckled.

"Enough of this discussion." Standing, Hudson waved

a hand toward the dance floor, hoping Melody didn't think he sounded like a spoiled rich kid. But he probably was. "There's some good music playing, and I've got a beautiful woman to dance with."

"I'll definitely take the dancing over the skydiving or racing cars." Melody stood.

Hudson chuckled as he held out his hand. "While we dance, maybe I can change your mind." When Melody put her hand in his, the rush he felt was as good as skydiving or speeding around an oval track. How had this woman triggered his interest in such a short time? He'd better be careful or he'd be jumping without a parachute. His experience with Nicole had taught him caution when it came to women.

"Hardly. I don't have to leave the ground when dancing."

"Then, you've never danced the jitterbug with me."

"Not something I plan to do in this evening gown."

"Probably not." Hudson put an arm around her as they joined the other couples dancing to a slow romantic tune.

She looked up at him. "I have to let you know the last time I danced was at Ian and Annie's wedding."

"Never fear. Just follow my lead."

"Easier said than done. I'm not used to following."

"Somehow I knew that." Smiling, Hudson guided Melanie across the dance floor.

"You *do* dance very well."

"I should. I had enough lessons when I was a kid. While the other boys were out playing ball, I was gliding around Miss Smithers' dance studio with some girl I didn't like and hating every minute."

Melody laughed. "Must've been rough being you."

Happy to make her laugh, Hudson let the sound wind

its way into his heart. "It's always been tough being me. I was the youngest kid with three older sisters. Three. They ganged up on me constantly."

"But they must've been a window into the lives of women."

"I never thought of it that way." Hudson shook his head. "I should've taken notes, but sadly I didn't. I was too young to appreciate the knowledge I could've gained. I was merely a nuisance to my older sisters."

"I can see that."

"You wound me, and here I thought you were a kind person."

She laughed again, and the sound filled his chest with warmth. He pulled her a little closer as another slow number started. For a few moments they danced without talking. He hadn't felt this unguarded in years. This was one date he wished didn't have to end.

Chapter Two

Nothing had prepared Melody for her attraction to Hudson Conrick. Did she believe in love at first sight? Never. How had that crazy question popped into her mind? With everything she had to think about tonight, her mind must be playing tricks on her. Sure he was handsome, a good dancer and a gentleman, but he also liked to skydive and race cars. Who knew what other crazy things he liked to do? No way could she be having romantic feelings about a man she'd met only a few hours ago.

Attraction at first sight was plausible but not love.

The music faded, and Melody gazed up at him. "I apologize, but I have to check with Adam about the silent auction now."

"I'll tag along if you don't mind."

"Sure." Melody found it difficult to concentrate with Hudson by her side. Thankfully, the meeting with Adam lasted only a few minutes. As Melody and Hudson returned to their table, they received a few speculative glances from a couple of her coworkers, but she ignored them. She didn't want to add to the conjecture.

While the band played a lively number, Hudson tapped

his foot. "Can I convince you to dance again, or do we have to stick to the slow dances?"

Melody gripped the back of her chair as if it was a life-saver in the sea of her own uncertainty. Would she encourage his interest if she agreed? This date contained no future commitment, and he certainly expected to dance with his date. Enjoying this time was what she needed to do, but she couldn't let her attraction to Hudson show.

"You seem dubious."

Melody's halfhearted smile skidded into a grimace. Did she dare say what she was thinking? "Most of the men I know, including my brothers, don't like to dance."

Hudson held out his hands. "Hey, what can I say? I have to make use of those lessons."

Melody couldn't help laughing. "Okay. I wouldn't want them to go to waste."

Hudson grabbed her hand. "And we wouldn't want to waste this good music, either."

Letting the music and Hudson whirl her away, she focused on the here and now. She wouldn't think about the future, and she wouldn't think about the past. Tonight she would live in the moment and relish every aspect of it.

The time with Hudson sped like one of his race cars. When the band announced the last dance, she couldn't believe the evening was about to end. Despite her vow only to think about the present, had she let herself get too involved?

No. Tonight wouldn't translate into anything for tomorrow. One and done like her other blind dates. That philosophy kept her heart safe from disappointment.

Hudson escorted her off the dance floor. "Do you have any last-minute things you have to do?"

"I do. I'll check with Adam to see if they have a job for me before I leave. I hope you don't mind waiting."

"Not at all. I'll get your things and meet you there."

"Thanks." Melody hurried to the back of the room where Adam and Annie sat at a long table.

As Melody drew nearer, Annie looked up, a little frown creasing her brow. "What are you doing here? You should be with your handsome date."

Glancing at the pile of receipts, Melody ignored Annie's reference to Hudson. "I thought you might need me for something."

Annie shook her head. "Got it under control, and you're going to like my report on Monday. Now get out of here and enjoy the rest of your evening."

"Okay." Melody went around the table and gave Annie a hug. "Thanks for all you've done."

"You're welcome. Now go, go, go." Annie shooed Melody away with her hands. "You have a date to take care of."

"Okay, okay. I'm off."

When Melody turned, Hudson was standing a few feet away as he held her purse and wrap. A momentary image of Christopher flashed through her mind. Hudson didn't resemble her former fiancé in the least. Christopher had been shorter with light brown hair and blue eyes. So why had his image come to mind when she looked at Hudson? She couldn't begin to answer that question.

She tried to shake off the pain in her heart. Thoughts of her old love usually didn't bring as much hurt these days, and she thought of him less often. No one could ever replace Christopher. He'd been her life, and now he was gone. Her only comfort lay in knowing she would see him again in heaven.

"Ready to leave?" Hudson's question snapped her out of her sentimental thoughts.

Melody nodded. "Annie assures me that I'm not needed here."

"Good. I've called James. He should have the car at the front door when we get there."

"James? Really?"

"Yeah. That's his name." A frown puckered Hudson's eyebrows as they entered the lobby.

Melody shrugged. "When I was a kid we used say, 'Home, James,' to my dad when my brothers and I were strapped into our car seats in the back and we were pretending that he was our chauffeur."

"Oh, I see." Hudson stood aside as Melody scooted through the door ahead of him.

He probably didn't see the same humor that she saw. He didn't have to pretend to have a chauffeur. Why had she told Hudson that story? It only underscored the differences between them.

The inadequate feeling she thought she'd overcome slithered through her mind. She tried to push the unwelcome thoughts away, but they kept intruding. She remembered how the popular rich girls had befriended her, and she'd been on top of the world. But they'd made her the butt of their jokes. The reality of the situation had been a cruel awakening.

As a grown woman, she was stupid to let old hurts color her perception. But that incident popped into her thoughts more often than she would like. Once they were settled in the limousine, Hudson poured himself another glass of water. He raised his eyebrows as he gazed at her. "Would you like one?"

She nodded, her mouth parched. For a minute, they

sipped their water in silence. What was he thinking? What did it matter? Even though she didn't plan to go out with him again, she wanted this date to have been a success.

"So you have brothers?" After the silence, his question sounded like a loud clap in an empty room.

Melody pushed aside the cobwebs of her thoughts. "Yeah, younger brothers."

"How many?"

Melody never knew how to respond when people asked that question. Fortunately, it didn't come up that often. A lump rose in her throat as she thought about her eldest brother, Blake, who'd been killed when his dirt bike had skidded and slammed into a tree.

"Is that a question I shouldn't have asked?" He peered at her in the dim light, concern on his face.

Waiting for her emotions to subside, she shook her head. "The eldest of my brothers died in a dirt bike accident when he was seventeen. He was a year younger than me. I have two other brothers. So I never know quite how to answer that question."

"I'm sorry about your brother. That must've been a difficult time."

"Thanks. It was for my whole family." Melody lowered her gaze as she twisted the strap on her purse. She didn't want to talk about it anymore, or she was afraid she might embarrass herself by bursting into tears. She'd lost too many men in her life.

Her brother. Her father. Her fiancé.

Hudson fell silent again, and Melody stared out the window as the limo turned onto her street. The evening was at its close, but she didn't want it to end on a sad note. She had to say something cheery or at least make an attempt. "I appreciate you taking me to the fund-raiser. I had a good time."

The concern on Hudson's face morphed into a lazy smile. "Me, too. It's been a while since I've been able to show off my dancing skills."

Melody laughed, feeling the earlier sadness waft away. "Ms. Smithers would be proud."

Hudson joined in the laughter. "Maybe. I don't believe she ever considered me one of her star pupils. I stepped on too many toes."

"She should've seen you tonight."

"Thanks." He set his empty glass on the bar, then turned to her. "I had more than a great time tonight. I enjoyed every minute with you. I'd like to take you out to dinner next Saturday."

Melody's heart caught in her throat. His request caught her off guard. Aware that she'd upped his expectations with her compliments, she wished he hadn't asked. How could she explain her reasons for not wanting to go out with him again? She didn't want to go into past heartaches that he couldn't begin to understand. Could he possibly see how their very different backgrounds weren't compatible? "I did have a fun time with you, but another date wouldn't be a good idea. I'm sorry."

His eyebrows knit above his brown eyes. "Why not? It's only dinner."

"I don't know, Hudson." Melody sighed. "I'm not sure I fit into your world."

The limousine came to a stop in front of her house before Hudson could respond to her statement. He lowered the window between them and the driver. "James, we're going to sit here for a minute." Without waiting for

James's reply, Hudson turned back to her. "My world isn't any different from yours."

Shaking her head, Melody let out a halfhearted chuckle. "You come from a rich family. I'm from small-town Georgia and grew up poor. I went to the University of Georgia on a HOPE scholarship, got a degree in psychology and then a masters in counseling. I worked for a few years with a government job-counseling center before I started working at The Village. I love my work there. What do I know about the life of a multi-millionaire?"

"Maybe you should find out. People are people. How can you make a judgment without getting to know me?"

"I don't want to go down a road that wouldn't be good for either of us. Tonight was wonderful, but this has to be it." Melody gritted her teeth, wishing he would listen to reason, but his mentioning her judgment went right to her guilt. Was she too critical? But this wasn't all about his money. She couldn't forget his love of skydiving and car races—dangerous activities that took lives. She couldn't be with a man who took such risks.

"I won't take no for an answer."

"Please don't make this difficult. It's not just because you come from wealth and I don't. You like to live on the edge and I like to play it safe. How can that be a good combination?"

"It might be fun to find out."

Melody let out an exasperated sigh. "You don't give up, do you?"

"Not when I want something." Hudson's look could cut steel. "I won't press you anymore tonight, but you haven't heard the last of me, Ms. Hammond."

"I'll take that as a warning, Mr. Conrick."

"James, I'll be walking Ms. Hammond to the door."

Again the driver seemed to materialize out of thin air. He opened the door. Hudson stepped out and extended his hand to Melody. She braced herself against her reaction to his touch as she took his hand. She didn't want to like the way her hand felt in his, but she did. She didn't want to like anything about tonight, but she did. She didn't want to think about Hudson kissing her good-night, but she did. She couldn't let that kiss happen, no matter what she wanted.

When they stepped onto her porch, Melody quickly snatched her keys from her purse and unlocked her door. She turned to look up at him, another lump forming in her throat. Her head was telling her to run and run fast, but her heart told her to take a chance. She couldn't listen to her heart. "I can't thank you enough for being my escort and for your support."

That lazy smile reappeared. "Sure you can. You can go out with me again."

Melody clenched her fist around her purse strap. She would not give in. She would stand her ground no matter how captivating his smile was. She would not take a chance on another man determined to pursue something dangerous, especially when it had no redeeming value. "I'm sorry, Hudson. The answer is no. Please don't ask me again."

"I'm not going to make promises I can't keep." Hudson leaned closer, almost close enough to kiss her.

"Thanks again. Good night." Her heart pounding, she ducked inside as his good-night was lost in the closing of her door.

Melody watched through the sidelight window while Hudson strode away without a backward glance. Her

wobbly legs failed to move an inch. She put her fingertips to her lips where he'd almost planted a kiss. Her
pulse raced as she stood there until the taillights of the
limousine faded from her view. She couldn't let his per-
suasive words, his handsome face or his generous nature
change her determination not to go out with him again.

The redbrick buildings of the former college gave
a stately air to The Village of Hope campus. Even the
grays of winter didn't take away from the beauty as Hudson parked his car near the administration offices. How
would Melody react when she saw him? He'd spent the
past four days trying not to think about her, but her image
plagued his thoughts.

Maybe his ego had taken a hit when she'd refused to
go out with him again. He wasn't used to women turning him down. But he was wary of female motives no
matter the circumstances. Too often they were looking
at his bank account and not at him. Melody certainly
had reason to see him as a dollar sign even if her interest wasn't personal.

He wanted another date with her, and he would find a
way to get one. But first, he had other things to accomplish. After a little research, he'd discovered that they
were still taking bids for the women's shelter project.
Winning that bid was his goal.

Hudson and Carter Duncan, the general manager and
numbers guy from the construction division of Conrick
Industries, walked into the impressive reception area
with its shiny marble floor and the two-story ceiling. A
smiling silver-haired woman sat behind the massive reception desk. "Good morning. May I help you?"

"Good morning, Lovie. I'm Hudson Conrick, and this

is my colleague, Carter Duncan." Hudson motioned toward the short stocky man with the thinning brown hair who stood nearby. "We have an appointment with Adam Bailey and Melody Hammond."

Lovie's brow wrinkled. "How do you know my name?"

Hudson pointed toward the little gold bar pinned to her jacket. "It says so right there on your name tag."

Lovie shook her head. "You can't fool me. You said my name before you were close enough to read it."

"Okay. You've got me." Hudson chuckled. "I heard about you and your quilt the other night at the fund-raiser."

Clapping her hands together, Lovie beamed. "So wonderful what the Lord can do with a little bit of nothing."

"I saw your quilt. That wasn't a little bit of nothing. It was a lot of work. A true work of art and love." Hudson leaned on the raised counter of the reception desk.

"Thank you. I am proud of it and so happy I was able to help The Village." Lovie blushed as she reached for the phone. "I'll let Adam know you're on your way to his office, which is down the hallway to the left."

"Thanks." Hudson nodded, then fell into step with Carter as they made their way around the corner.

"I sure hope you know what you're doing. I wouldn't want to make your father unhappy with this venture." Carter frowned as he slowed his step and turned to Hudson.

Hudson stopped, taking in the worry in Carter's eyes. "I told you this project will be mine. I'm prepared to take this whole endeavor on my shoulders. You don't have to be concerned about a thing."

"I'll hold you to that."

"Your part is to help me get the numbers I need. I want

to be armed with as much information as possible when I confront my father."

Carter shook his head as they continued on their way. "Better you than me. Besides, I'd sure like it if this project saved my job."

Their footsteps sounded loud in the quiet hallway as Hudson tried not to think about his dad's reaction to this undertaking. He had heard rumors that the construction side of the business wasn't doing well. Carter's statement made it a certainty. Hudson would like nothing better than to save the jobs of all those involved. Before they reached their destination, Adam stepped into the hallway. "Good to see you again, Mr. Conrick."

Hudson shook hands, then made introductions. Adam ushered them into his office. Hudson glanced around the Spartan space until his gaze rested on Melody. Although she smiled as she greeted them, she didn't look happy to be there. Was she still wishing to avoid him?

Adam motioned for them to sit on the black leather chairs near his desk. "I understand you want to see the blueprints for the new project and tour the area. Is that correct?"

Hudson nodded as he shrugged out of his jacket and hung it over the back of the chair. "Carter here is my numbers man. He'll want to see what you've got so Conrick Construction can give you a bid."

"We're close to making a decision, so you'll have to give us your proposal by Monday." Adam pushed the rolls of blueprints and another folder across the desk.

"That won't be a problem." Despite the statement, Hudson's dry mouth and racing pulse gave him no peace. So much of what he wanted to prove to his father was riding on this proposal. For years he'd walked the path his father had set before him. Those dance lessons, law school and the army had been his father's command. Hudson was determined not to jump to his dad's wishes anymore. Staring death in the face on the battlefield made him realize he'd been living a life that had been chosen for him. He didn't know who he was or what he wanted because he'd let someone else plan his life. Not anymore.

Could he make his case? No time for doubts. He would finally stand up for himself and make his own mark in this world. That included his interest in one very reluctant woman. Melody Hammond was a challenge he couldn't resist.

While thoughts of standing up to his father rolled through Hudson's mind, Carter studied the blueprints and the information Adam had provided. Finally, he closed the folder and glanced at Hudson. "I'd like to take these blueprints to the construction site."

Adam waved a hand in Melody's direction. "Melody will give you a tour. I have another meeting this morning, so I'll meet you in the senior center after you finish."

Melody produced another uncomfortable smile as she led Hudson and Carter into the hallway. "Let me stop by my office and grab my coat."

"Sure." Hudson nodded as he walked beside her. "It's a little chilly out there today, unlike the night of the fundraiser."

She nodded, still trying to hold her smile in place as she scurried into her office and out of sight. Had he made a mistake in mentioning their date? He had to quit second-guessing himself. Women didn't usually intimidate him, but Melody did. He'd never met a woman like her.

"I can see why you're eager to do this project. She's quite a looker."

Annoyed at Carter's description of Melody, Hudson glared at the other man. "She might be good-looking, but this isn't about her. This is about business."

"If you say so." Grinning, Carter shrugged.

Hudson balled and unballed his hand. The urge to wipe that smile off Carter's face passed through Hudson's thoughts. Not wise. Not productive. Not Christian.

He took a deep breath as Melody reappeared wearing a dark gray trench coat. With a nod, she led them out the side door. The bright sunshine belied the temperature outside. Hudson liked the way sunlight sparkled in her blond hair as it lay on the jacket's dark material. He wished he could say something to brighten her mood, but it was obvious his presence didn't make her happy. Much the same as the night of the fund-raiser, Melody charged ahead at a fast clip as she made her way across the quad. She walked with determination. He liked that about her, too. When she reached the fountain, she stopped and turned. "I'll show you our current women's facility so you can see what's been done before with an existing building."

"Works for me." Carter nodded.

Hudson nodded but didn't say anything. He wanted to ask about the colored water and balloons on the fountain but decided against it. The less he said the better at this point. The situation demanded patience. Not one of his virtues. He'd let Carter take the lead. That might be more to Melody's liking.

Melody took one of the sidewalks leading away from the fountain toward the right side of the quad. She said little until they reached the building, where she punched in a code on the pad next to the door. Looking up at Carter, she motioned for him to go in. "We hold security very important, especially for our women. So we require background checks on every member of your crew if you win the bid for this project."

Without a word, Carter entered the building and Hudson followed, walking along the hallway where the faint smell of a pine-scented cleaning solution explained the gleaming tile floors. "Nice facility you have here."

"Thanks." Melody turned her head, giving him the first genuine smile of the day. "This used to be a dormitory that we converted into apartments. There are a dozen on each floor. That's what we plan to do with the other building. That's why I wanted to start here."

"Your new project's similar to this one?" Hudson asked.

"Yes." Melody stepped toward the first door. "I've made arrangements for you to look at this apartment. The resident gave her permission to let me show the place while she's attending job training. You're welcome to look around."

Carter made a hurried trip through the place while Hudson took a more leisurely stroll, observing the modest furnishings in the two-bedroom dwelling. When he finished his tour, he joined Carter, who was studying the blueprints he'd laid out on the dinette table near the galley kitchen.

Hudson glanced at Melody. "Do they all have the same layout?"

"Basically." Melody shifted her weight from foot to foot as her gaze flitted around the room. "Are you ready to see the other building?"

"Absolutely," Carter said as he rolled up the blueprint.

Minutes later, as Melody reached the door to the next building, she turned, focusing her attention on Carter.

Hudson didn't want to believe that she was doing her best to ignore him, but he couldn't dismiss the evidence.

"When we go in, you'll see that the interior has been gutted. It's been that way for a couple of years. We'd planned to renovate it right after we did the other one, but we didn't have the funds at the time. So we put this one on hold."

Hudson digested this information as Melody granted them access. He glanced around at the bare concrete block walls and floors illuminated with light filtering through dingy windows. He tried to focus on the possibilities rather than the grim picture the place presented while Carter asked the questions. Hudson figured the less he said the better.

After they completed the tour, Melody locked up, then turned to face them. "Do you have more questions for me?"

"Not right now, but I may have some after I go over the information I've collected today." Carter stuck the rolled-up blueprints under his arm.

Melody produced one of those forced smiles. "Good. Then we'll meet with Adam."

While they walked back across the quad, she chatted comfortably with Carter. The breeze ruffled her blond hair around her shoulders as she laughed at something he said. Why couldn't she be that comfortable with him? She obviously wanted to make it abundantly clear that she meant what she'd told him the night of the fundraiser. She wouldn't go out with him again. Would that be a strike against Conrick Construction getting the bid?

Hudson shook that question away as they walked into the senior center cafeteria. The folks here at The Village would make a sound business decision based on the bids they received. Not on personal feelings.

Melody introduced them to the woman who signed them in. Another layer of security. Immediately, Adam joined them and led them to a nearby table.

"Do you have questions for me now that you've seen the building we want to renovate?" Adam asked.

Hudson leaned back and steepled his fingers as he placed his elbows on the arms of the chair. "Melody has explained your emphasis on security, so will we have access to a construction entrance for our heavy equipment?"

"I'm glad you brought up that point. When we did the first renovations, we didn't have any residents so we didn't have to worry about security." Adam wrinkled his brow. "We have an emergency entrance on the road that runs along the back side of the campus. It's there for vehicles that are unable to go through the main gate. I'm sure we can make some arrangements to use it if the need arises."

Melody scooted forward in her chair and frowned. "Do you think it'll be necessary to use that?"

Despite her frown, Hudson relished her question. At least, she was talking to him. "I wanted to cover all the bases. The logistics will figure into our bid. I know how important security is to you."

A little smile tugged at the corners of her mouth. "Yeah, it is. So opening another entrance worries me."

"I understand. If we get the bid, I'll be personally responsible for personnel and vehicles that go through there if we have to use it." Hudson watched her expression as she took in his response.

"I appreciate that, and I'll hold you to it." The look in

her brown eyes let him know that she meant business. "We can't be too careful when it comes to the women here. They depend on us for their safety."

Hudson tried to put himself in the place of the women who had fled abusive situations and the fear they must feel.

"Does that cover everything?" Adam asked.

Nodding, Carter looked Hudson's way as he tapped the roll of blueprints. "I've got everything I need."

"Great." Adam stood. "You're welcome to join us for lunch."

"Sounds good to me." Hudson nodded as he glanced at Melody. He breathed a sigh of relief when she didn't make some excuse to leave.

Carter stood. "I appreciate the invitation, but I've got to get back to the office. We'll have that bid to you by the deadline."

Hudson popped up from his chair. "I'll be right back after I see Carter to the exit."

"Good to meet you. I look forward to seeing your bid." Adam shook Carter's hand, then turned to Hudson. "We'll wait here for you."

"Thanks." Hudson fell into step beside Carter. "So what do you think?"

"We can come up with a competitive bid, but I'm not sure it'll meet muster with that pretty blonde. What did you do to get on her bad side?" Carter gave Hudson a speculative glance.

"Hard telling. I'm not going to worry about her."

Carter narrowed his gaze. "I thought you wanted this project because of her."

"I told you before she's not the reason for my interest in this. Showing my dad that I can be my own man is on top of the list." Hudson clapped Carter on the back. "We'll talk after you've had a chance to crunch the numbers. Thanks for your work."

Hudson hurried back to the table. He didn't miss Melody's less-than-enthusiastic smile upon his return, but he wouldn't let that dampen his spirit.

As they went through the cafeteria line, Hudson took in Melody's interaction with those around her. She had a smile for the workers and knew them by name. What did he need to do to gain one of those smiles? Maybe he should quit thinking about himself. That might be a start in the right direction.

For too many years, he'd lived his life, never understanding the plight of folks less fortunate than himself. Even though his parents had always been charity minded, he hadn't known how other people lived until he'd joined the army. Looking back, he could see his father's wisdom when he'd insisted that Hudson spend time in the military. The experience had given him a new perspective on life and the world.

Could Melody appreciate that, or would she continue to look at him as a person who was out of touch with the people she served? He'd done himself no favors the night of the fund-raiser when he'd jokingly talked about attending the event to please his father. At the beginning of the evening, he'd had no idea that he'd find Melody a very fascinating woman. Now he had to work doubly hard to undo her bad impression of him. No easy task. And if she did show an interest in him, would it be for him or the money he could contribute to her cause? When it came to women, that thought was never far from the surface.

After they brought their food to the table, Adam offered a prayer of thanks. For a few minutes, they ate without saying anything, the sounds of lively conversation flowing around them. Hudson observed the residents of the senior center as they partook of their meals. The place radiated with joy. This was a happy place—one he wanted to help. And he wanted to help one very independent woman, but he wasn't sure she wanted it.

Hudson set down his fork. "The residents here seem to be having a good time."

Melody nodded. "We do our best to make this a wonderful place to live. Ian does a great job with the facility."

"That's right," Adam said to Hudson. "In fact, he's got one of the most anticipated events of the year for the senior center coming up. The Valentine banquet. We can always use some volunteers for that. Would you be interested?"

Hudson let the request roll through his mind as he watched the consternation spread across Melody's face. She wasn't happy about Adam's suggestion. Was this a chance to prove to her that he was willing to help others? "What kind of volunteers do you need?"

"Adam, Ian probably has enough helpers." Melody wrinkled her brow. "He usually invites the youth group from his dad's church to act as servers, and we always have plenty of people from right here. You don't need to be bothering Hudson."

Adam nodded. "That's true, but it never hurts to let other folks see what we're doing. What do you say, Hudson?"

"It sounds like a great opportunity. I'll talk to Ian and see where he can use my services." He'd love to help out where he could, and if this was another way to spend more time with Melody Hammond, then things were looking up.

Chapter Three

The two-story cream-colored stucco house with the stone accents spread out across the piney woods landscape like a small hotel. Hudson surveyed the structure as he parked his car in the circular drive. Melody would probably consider the residence a place of excess. He'd seen her reaction when he'd shown up in a limo. But that had been his best option. He'd thought to spare her from trying to get in and out of his sports car in a dress or having to clamber over the junk in his SUV. And after he'd seen her gown, he knew he'd made the right decision.

Melody probably thought he lived a life of luxury and didn't understand the plight of the people she helped every day. What would it take to convince her that having money was a good thing? Making money was something he was good at, and he intended to keep doing it. Did that make him a bad guy? He wanted to show her how his wealth could help her beyond her fund-raising.

But first he had to convince his dad that doing the construction for The Village was a valuable thing.

Loping toward the front porch, Hudson formulated the speech he hoped would convince his father. Hudson strode through the house until he reached the office at the far end of the first floor. Armed with Carter's facts and figures, Hudson knocked on the dark oak-paneled door.

"Come in." H. P. Conrick's deep voiced boomed from the other side.

Hudson pushed open the door. "Hey, Dad."

"Hello, son. What can I do for you today?"

"I've got a project to run by you."

H.P. motioned toward the chair next to his cherry-inlaid mahogany desk. "Have a seat."

As he made himself comfortable, Hudson studied his father and tried to gauge his mood. With his silver-gray hair and trim physique, H.P. was a commanding figure, even a little intimidating. Hudson took a deep breath and then started to explain the details of his bid on the women's shelter project at The Village. His father appeared to be listening intently but with a skeptical attitude.

"Why is this so important to you? Does it have anything to do with a pretty blonde?"

Hudson knit his eyebrows together. "Why would you say that?"

H.P.'s laughter echoed through the room. "The Clarks mentioned seeing you with a lovely young lady in a red dress. They were quite impressed with her."

Had this information reached his mother's ears? She would be all over it—her matchmaking antennae at full strength. Hudson couldn't deny an interest in Melody, but when it came to women, *caution* was his operative word. He wasn't about to fall into the trap of women who used him for his wealth again, no matter how appealing Melody Hammond might be. He wanted to get to know her in his own time and see what kind of person lay behind her pretty face.

"Melody's in charge of the women's ministries at The Village, and this is a cause Conrick Industries can get behind—good PR for the company and a worthy cause, too." Hudson squared his shoulders. "I want to be in charge of this endeavor."

H.P. wrinkled his brow. "Ridiculous. You've not worked on the construction side of the business for years. Why would you think you're qualified to be in charge?"

Doubts crowded Hudson's mind, but he shoved them aside. "It's true I haven't been involved in that part of the business since before I was in the army, but it's still my first love when it comes to Conrick Industries."

"I've nearly decided to divest the construction portion of the business. It's too volatile and hasn't produced substantial income in recent years." H.P. stood and pounded his desk, his voice raised. "And now you're asking me to practically give away our services. I won't do that no matter how good the publicity."

Hudson hoped his dad wouldn't blow up. "Do you have a prospective buyer?"

"No, but I'll close it down if I can't find one. Better than pouring money into a losing proposition."

"What about the people who work there? They'll lose their jobs."

H.P. knit his shaggy eyebrows. "Hard business decisions must be made."

"Let me take it off your hands."

H.P. sat on the front of his desk and narrowed his gaze. "You want to take over a business that's struggling to survive?"

The consequences of failure swirled through Hudson's thoughts. What would he prove to his dad if he didn't succeed? Hudson wanted to strike out on his own, and the perfect opportunity had just materialized. "I do. I'll take it as my part of the inheritance. You can draw up the papers, and I won't expect another thing from your will."

His dad pushed himself away from the desk and began pacing back and forth across the black, gold and cream colored design in the Oriental rug. Finally, he stopped, disapproval radiating from his eyes. "It can't happen. That's not what I have planned for you."

Hudson took a deep breath. "Dad, I've told you before. I don't want to take over the family business—"

"You don't have a choice." H.P. glared at Hudson.

"Elizabeth wants the job. She's worked at the company and is well qualified. She has an MBA to go along with her talent. Her kids are grown, and she could devote her time to the business. She'd be the perfect one to step into your shoes when you decide to retire."

"No. Do you understand me? You're going to do as I say and take over the company. Your sister's not as well versed as you."

"Only because you resisted letting her learn the ropes." Hudson stood and went to the window that looked out on the piney woods running up to the expanse of barely green lawn. What would it take to change his father's mind? He turned, trying to keep his cool in the wake of his father's displeasure. "You have a few years to teach her everything you know. She's smart, and she's good at what she does. It's been her dream to step into your shoes since she was two."

With a glower on his face, H.P. joined Hudson at the window. "What do you mean since she was two?"

Hudson strode over to the built-in bookcases that covered a whole wall and picked up a photo frame that contained a collage. He pointed to the photo in one corner. "See."

A begrudging smile crept across his dad's face as he studied the photo of his eldest daughter wearing his shoes when she was a toddler. Shaking his head, he narrowed his gaze as he looked at Hudson. "I don't care what you say. A Conrick son takes over for the father. That's the way it's always been done, and that's the way it'll stay."

"If something will work better doing it a different way, don't you change instead of sticking with the old way?"

H.P. gave Hudson a begrudging nod. "I suppose."

"Dad, bring the company into the twenty-first century. Let Elizabeth take over."

"You're wasting your breath if you think you can change my mind." H.P. boomed his annoyance.

"For now, will you at least let me run the construction division?" Hudson held his breath, waiting for his dad's reaction.

"If you do, I'll expect you to make money. I won't tolerate losses."

"And there won't be any." Hudson wished he could be sure of that statement. Was he stepping out on a limb that wouldn't hold him?

"Are you still involved in that skydiving stuff—a frivolous pursuit?"

"What's a frivolous pursuit?" Hudson's mother walked into the room.

"Susan, talk some sense into your son." H.P. greeted his wife with a kiss on the cheek.

"My son? I thought he was your son, too." Susan gave Hudson a hug.

"Well, right now I'm wondering about that." H.P.

looped an arm around his wife's shoulders. "He's bucking the family tradition."

"Do I need to act as referee between you two again?" Susan smiled up at her husband.

"No, just talk some sense into him."

Susan looked over at Hudson. "Can you stay for lunch?"

Hudson wondered whether his mother could help his dad see the wisdom of granting Elizabeth her wish. Maybe his dad needed a woman's point of view. "Yeah."

"Excellent. We're having some of Sarah's chili. It's simmering on the stove as we speak." Susan slipped an arm through her husband's and paraded him to the door.

Watching his parents, Hudson followed. They were a happy couple, with a very traditional marriage where his mother, unlike his sisters, worked inside the home. Still fit for her age and still young looking thanks to the hairdresser who made sure she stayed a brunette rather than a graying matriarch, his mom was a pampered Southern belle with a housekeeper, cook and gardener. She spent her time doing church charity functions or community service, besides playing tennis and golf weekly when the weather permitted. Her charity activities should bode well for his efforts to help The Village.

When they reached the kitchen, Sarah, his parents' longtime cook, was busy at the stove. She turned to greet them. Her face lit up when she saw Hudson. She wiped her hands on a towel and hurried to greet him with a hug. "My favorite boy."

Hudson chuckled. "Sarah, you'd think one of these days you'd realize I'm grown up."

"Never." She laughed as she returned to the stove.

"Mom tells me you're serving us your famous chili."

Hudson remembered many a time when Sarah would sneak him cookies when he was a little boy.

"Absolutely, and the biggest serving is for you." She handed him an oversize bowl, steaming with the delicious mixture.

"Thanks." Hudson cradled it in his hands, the heat warming his heart. "Come join us."

Sarah shook her head. "Thanks, but I've already eaten, and I need to get dinner ready."

After Sarah served his parents, they found seats at the round oak table in the kitchen nook. H.P. gave thanks for the food, and they began eating in silence. Hudson wanted to bring up their earlier discussion but decided to wait for his father to start the conversation.

Setting down her spoon, Hudson's mother broke the silence. "What were you two arguing about?"

H.P. gave his wife an annoyed look. "We were having a discussion."

"True, but we're on opposite sides of the issue." Hudson nodded as he explained the situation.

"H.P., this time your son's right." Susan patted her husband's arm. "You can't push your kids into doing something they don't want to do. Give Hudson some freedom. Let him fly."

His father harrumphed. "What do you mean let him fly? He wants to skydive. What a waste of time."

"Give him wings to do what he chooses. He jumped out of planes to serve his country. He deserves to use that skill however he wants." Susan raised an eyebrow.

Hudson listened to his parents bicker back and forth about his future. He needed to stand up for himself rather than let his mother argue for him. "Dad, I've worked for you ever since I got out of the army. I've done your bidding. Now I'm going to chart my own path. I'd like your blessing to run the construction division, but if not, don't plan on me taking over Conrick Industries. Elizabeth can do that far better than I can."

A muscle worked in H.P.'s jaw. The silence in the room shouted louder than anything his father could have said. Hudson feared he could never convince his father that his sister deserved a chance to prove herself.

"Mr. C., you should listen to your son. Ms. Elizabeth is one smart lady." Sarah turned back to the stove.

A frown knitting his brow, H.P. glanced at her. Hudson held his breath, waiting for his father to boom out his disapproval. Instead, he set down his spoon and eyed Hudson. "You can't use these women to persuade me to turn things over to Elizabeth. You're a Conrick son, and you will run the company when I retire. However, I'll let you see what you can do with the construction division, but I'll reevaluate things in six months."

"Thanks, Dad. You won't be disappointed." Frustrated that he couldn't change his father's mind, Hudson had to make do with whatever opportunity he was offered for now.

"The bid from Conrick Construction wins my vote."

Melody's heart sank as Bob Franklin, chairman of the board for The Village, voiced his opinion. After their detailed discussion of each bid, how could she disagree with the three men who sat around the table with her?

"What do you think, Melody?" Ian raised his eyebrows as he looked her way.

Melody sighed. "I concur. They've given us the best bid."

"It's a good choice." Adam nodded. "I was impressed

when Mr. Conrick and Mr. Duncan came out to view the building. I believe we'll be happy with this choice."

A murmur of agreement went around the table as Melody resigned herself to working with Hudson. She'd prayed that God would lead the group to make the wisest decision, even if it meant hiring Hudson's company. She hoped he would honor her wishes and not push for another date, especially now that they would be associates on this project. As the head of Conrick Construction, how much would Hudson be involved with the day-to-day activities? She could hope not much, but something told her the chances were slim.

"Looks as though you have a phone call to make, Melody." Adam stood and pushed in his chair.

She grabbed her satchel from the floor. "After we have a signed contract bond, I'll send an email to everyone with a full report."

"Good job today." Bob Franklin shook hands with everyone, then accompanied Melody to the door and opened it for her. "I'll be looking for that report. Thanks."

She nodded and slipped down the hall to her office. Once inside, she leaned back against the door and closed her eyes. Now she had to call Hudson. With a heavy sigh, she made her way across the room and plopped onto her chair as she put her satchel on the desk. She extracted her phone and scrolled through her contacts until she came to his name.

She stared at the screen, willing herself to dial the number, but she couldn't do it yet. Instead, she bowed her head. She needed strength in order to make this call and not come across in a negative manner. This project was important to a lot of women who needed a safe place, and she couldn't let personal feelings jeopardize it in any way. *Lord, please give me wisdom where Hudson Conrick is concerned. Please provide me peace for this situation. Let me have a loving heart for all concerned.*

Taking a deep breath, Melody tapped the screen. The phone began to ring while her heart raced.

"Hudson Conrick."

His deep voice made Melody's heart beat even faster. "Hello, Mr. Conrick. This is Melody Hammond from The Village. I'm calling to let you know that we've decided to award Conrick Construction the contract for the women's shelter."

"That's great news! I'm looking forward to working with you on this very worthy project."

Melody wished she could say, "me, too," but it would be a lie. "Ian has prepared a contract bond for you or a representative from the company to sign."

"When would be a good time for me to meet with you?"

"Contact Ian. He's in charge of contracts."

"I will."

"When do you plan to start the work?" Melody wanted to prepare herself for Hudson's presence on campus.

"I hope to sign the contract today, and we'll get started as soon as the permits are in place."

"Good. So we'll talk after everything's ready." Melody ended the call, already eager for him to finish, so she wouldn't have to deal with him. But this was her project and she would see it through. She'd already spent a sleepless night thinking about today's decision. Now it was done.

She walked to the window and stared out at the quad. The sun glinted off the water cascading in the fountain. Bare-branched trees lifted their limbs into the blue sky.

The mild winter weather reminded her of the night she'd gone out with Hudson. She couldn't deny that she'd enjoyed the evening. It would be so easy to accept another date with him, but she couldn't let herself get tangled up with a man who liked to take chances, or a wealthy man who used his money and influence to get what he wanted.

Hudson was every bit that person.

But she knew she wasn't being fair to him. She couldn't go into the project with a negative attitude. Prayer. That was what she needed again. It had helped her through the phone conversation. It would help her again while she worked with him.

Lord, help me to see Hudson through Your eyes and not my own. Help us to have a good working relationship so this project can move forward in a way that is pleasing to You.

When she raised her head, she tried to analyze why she was on pins and needles. The answer wasn't hard to find. Hudson represented a temptation she wasn't sure she could resist, despite her fears. She would be strong and determined. She wouldn't succumb to his appeals no matter how attractive. Now she had things to do and didn't have time to worry about Hudson's presence on campus.

An hour later, completely absorbed in her paperwork, Melody jumped when a knock sounded on the door. "Come in."

Ian poked his head around the door. "I need a witness while Hudson signs the papers."

"Sure." Melody moved with deliberate slowness as she prepared to meet Hudson. When she walked into Ian's office, her calm preparation fled. Hudson's handsome face and lazy smile made her pulse thunder just like the night of their date.

"Hello, Melody."

She took a deep breath. "You got here quickly."

"Would I be in trouble if I told you I was in a hurry to see you?"

"You would probably be better off if you told me you were in a hurry to sign the contract bond."

His smile spread into a grin. "That, too."

Not daring to look at Ian, Melody headed toward her desk and wondered what he thought of Hudson's comments. "Okay. I'm ready to witness."

Hudson looked so at ease, and she was tied in knots for no reason at all—at least, any reason that made sense. Why was she letting him make her so nervous?

In a matter of minutes he'd put his signature on the front page and initialed the remaining ones. She signed, and Ian put his notary seal on the document.

"We're official." Ian shook hands with Hudson. "Congratulations again."

Ian pulled his cell phone from his pocket and looked at the screen. "It's almost time for lunch. Join me, and we can discuss the Valentine banquet."

"Sounds good." Hudson glanced in her direction. "You'll be coming, too, won't you?"

Melody let the invitation roll through her mind. She would look bad if she declined. She couldn't avoid interacting with Hudson in the days to come, so she might as well get used to having him around. Thankfully today Ian would act as a buffer. "Certainly. Let me get my purse and jacket in my office."

As Melody met the two men in the hallway, she said another prayer for peace of mind. When she looked up, Hudson was smiling at her as if he knew this lunch meeting wasn't to her liking. Or was that her imagination?

The future was going to be filled with a lot of prayer if today was any indication. "I'm ready."

Hudson fell into step beside her as she headed for the door. "Are you a runner?"

"No. Why do you ask?" She scooted through the door he held open.

"You're always in a hurry." He gave her a wry smile.

"I'm usually racing from one part of the campus to another. So I tend to walk fast."

"Yeah, I can hardly keep up with her." Ian chuckled. "Lovie's nicknamed her the Roadrunner."

"Do you like hiking?" Hudson asked.

"I've never hiked."

"You should try it."

"No time. We've got a women's shelter to build." Melody wondered whether Hudson was trying to draw her into some group activity that she couldn't bow out of gracefully. She kept hearing his words. *I won't press you anymore tonight, but you haven't heard the last of me, Ms. Hammond.* He was true to his word. Could she be true to hers? Hudson pointed toward the fountain as they walked by it. "What's the deal with the green water and balloons?"

"We have a sponsor for the fountain today." Melody stopped and looked up at the purple balloons waving in the breeze.

"What does that mean?" Hudson asked.

"Last year when The Village was in financial distress, we decided to offer people the opportunity to make a donation in order to decorate the fountain for a special occasion." Melody started walking again. "Today's sponsor is Brady Hewitt. You met him at the fund-raiser. He's engaged to Adam's daughter, Kirsten."

Hudson nodded. "I remember them."

"It's his grandmother's birthday. She's a resident in the assisted living facility, and she loves green and lavender."

Opening the door to the senior center, Ian eyed Hudson. "You should get to know Brady. You two have a few things in common. He was in the army and is a big car buff."

"Yeah, good to know another army guy. I could arrange a guys' night out—maybe a Hawks game."

Ian nodded. "I could go for that."

Melody took in the men's conversation with interest. Ian treated Hudson like any other guy he knew—not like someone who came from wealth and privilege. She ought to take a lesson from her friend and remember that God looked at the heart, not on the outward appearance or one's bank account.

"So I could sponsor this fountain if I wanted to?" Hudson looked her way, a twinkle in his eyes, as they made their way to the registration desk.

"Sure. Make a donation and one of the maintenance staff will decorate the fountain per your instructions." Melody refused to speculate about Hudson's thoughts. "You have something in mind?"

"I might. I'll think about it."

After the threesome signed in, they made their way through the cafeteria line, the two guys talking about cars and sports. When they reached the table, Hudson set his tray down, then pulled out a chair for her and helped her out of her jacket. Was he working to impress her? No. She already knew the answer.

He was a gentleman. She'd seen the evidence during their date. He didn't have to impress anyone. When he walked into a room, people took notice. The cafeteria ladies couldn't wait to serve him. Even the senior ladies smiled at him as he went by. Well, he could bask in the admiration of those other women. He didn't need hers.

"When do you plan to start the work?" Ian put his plate on the table.

"Carter's working on the permits." Hudson turned to Melody. "Would you like me to give thanks?"

"Go ahead." Melody bowed her head.

As soon as he finished the prayer, he looked up at her. "I'd like to have you show me that construction entrance before I leave if you have time."

"I can do that after lunch." Melody wasn't sure she was dressed for the trek to their emergency gate, but she would make the best of it. She wished she could push the job off on Ian, but he had a client coming after lunch.

"Great. If you have time, you could show me the rest of the campus, too."

"That's a good idea." Ian took a bite of his burger.

"One campus tour coming right up." Melody produced another smile that she was sure didn't disguise her displeasure at Ian's suggestion. Was he trying to push Hudson and her together? The answer was obvious. She should be used to this scenario by now. For the past two years, everyone on campus had been trying to match her up with every single guy they encountered. She thought if she agreed to these dates that people would quit finding them for her, but things had only gotten worse.

"Great." Hudson smiled. "I'm eager to get this project started. We're using a lot of veterans on the crew. Too many of them get out of the service and can't find good-paying jobs. So I want to help."

"How were you able to arrange this when you've been out of the country?" Ian asked.

"The construction division of Conrick Industries has always been where my heart lies. I've kept in touch with Carter, especially when I became aware of guys and gals coming home and not being able to find decent wages. I wanted him to hire as many of them as he could. It's been a bonus for both of us."

Melody digested Hudson's statement. He sounded more and more like a regular guy instead of an heir to a multimillion-dollar fortune. Had she been looking at him with a jaundiced eye? Yeah, but she'd seen how folks with money could pretend to be your friend, then stab you in the back. Her prior experiences made her wary, but she knew she shouldn't paint Hudson with the same broad brush.

Throughout the rest of the meal, the men fell into a discussion about Hudson's plans to take over Conrick Construction. Would she see him out in a hard hat, or would he sit back in a cushy office and give orders? Instinct told her he wouldn't be sitting behind a desk. When Hudson glanced her way, she didn't have to guess why he'd insisted she come along. He wanted her to know his plans.

She did. She would meet him coming and going for the foreseeable future. And he wasn't about to let her forget that date he wanted.

Chapter Four

Hudson joined Ian as he cleared his dishes from the table. "We got sidetracked talking about other things and never did discuss what I can do for the Valentine banquet."

Nodding, Ian chuckled. "We certainly did. Stop by my office after your tour, and we'll talk about it. I should be through with my client by then."

"Thanks. I will." They shook hands, then Hudson turned to Melody as Ian headed toward the door. "Ready?"

Melody gazed up at him, her face an emotionless mask. He liked it better when he could read her expression. Her quietness during lunch signaled her reluctance for this task. What could he do to put her at ease?

She waved her arm in a sweeping gesture. "Since you've seen the senior center, women's shelter and the administration offices, where would you like to start?"

"I'll let you lead the way." Hudson motioned for her to go ahead.

She grabbed her jacket and folded it over her arm. "I hope you're ready for some walking. We're going to cover a lot of territory."

"And at a fast clip."

She turned to him with an annoyed look. "If you want a tour, you must keep up with the tour guide."

"Do I dare call you Ms. Roadrunner?" Hudson chuckled.

"Not if you want a tour." Melody pressed her lips together, but she couldn't hold back the smile that put a tiny curve on her pretty mouth.

"Okay, I'll behave."

"We'll start with the nursing home down this corridor." Melody forged ahead.

Smiling to himself, Hudson hurried to match her steps. She made quick work of the nursing home tour as she introduced him to several nurses and aides and reintroduced him to Brady Hewitt and Kirsten Bailey.

She then raced by the women's shelter until they came to two cul-de-sacs where a dozen modest houses sat. "These are our children's homes. Each one has room for six children and their house parents. On the weekends, it's not unusual to see kids running all over the quad while they play some kind of ball game. They often visit the residents in our senior center. The older folks love that, and the kids do, too."

"I'm sure they do. Every kid needs an older person as a friend." Their talk triggered memories of his maternal grandparents, Memaw and Papaw, and Sunday afternoons at their house—the fun and love—the big lawn where they'd played games. He shook the recollections away. He had to concentrate on one Melody Hammond and what she had to say.

"That's the beauty of this place. The kids have built-in grandparents. We definitely encourage it." Melody hurried ahead but stopped when she reached the fountain. "This is one of my favorite spots on campus."

"I can see why. The sound of the water is joyful like the events these decorations celebrate." Hudson tugged on one of the cords tying a balloon to the fountain, making it bob up and down.

Melody gave him a curious glance. "That's something I wouldn't expect to hear from you."

Hudson shrugged. "Why? I can be a sentimental guy."

"Somehow that doesn't fit a man who likes to race cars and jump out of planes." She didn't wait for his response but pointed toward the far end of the quad. "My other favorite spot is the Chapel Church."

"I can guess which building that is. That's one impressive steeple. Does it have a bell?"

"It does." Melody gave him an impish grin. "If you're really good, I'll take you up and let you look at it. There's a marvelous view of the campus from up there."

"What exactly constitutes really good?" Hudson raised his eyebrows.

She crossed her arms and stared at him. "Not asking the tour guide questions she can't answer."

Hudson laughed. "I'll try not to."

"Good. Then, you'll see something lots of folks never see."

"Do I dare ask another question?"

Melody shrugged. "Your choice."

Hudson craned his neck as he looked up to the cross that rose above the treetops. "You mean to tell me that the woman who likes to play it safe is willing to climb to the top of that steeple?"

Shaking her head, Melody stepped onto the church portico. "Don't make fun. It's very safe."

Hudson followed. "I couldn't help teasing you a little. Does that take me off the good list?"

"I'll let it go this time, but don't let it happen again."
Melody put her hand on the door handle, trying to hold
a serious expression in place.

"I see that smile trying to escape."

She couldn't suppress the upward curving of her
mouth. "Okay, you got me."

"I'm glad to see you smile. I don't want to be in trouble with you."

"And why is that?"

"You don't want to hear the reason."

She nodded. "Okay. We'll leave it at that."

"Good." He reached around and opened the door, their
shoulders brushing.

Without a word, she scurried inside. Quiet hovered
over the pews as Hudson followed her down the carpeted
aisle. Sunlight illuminated the stained glass windows.
The beauty inspired and lifted his spirit.

"I like to come here when the place is empty." She
spoke in hushed tones as she stopped halfway to the front.

"I can see why this is one of your favorite places," he
replied, his voice equally quiet.

"You should come to church here sometime." As soon
as the words were out of her mouth, her expression told
him she wished she could snatch them back.

Hudson looked at her with a grin. "You can count
on it."

She turned away without responding to him and
headed for a door on one side of the platform at the front.
"Through this entrance is the stairway to the bell tower."

"Lead the way." He followed her up the winding stair-
case until they came to another door.

"The bell's in here." She turned the knob and let the

dark wooden door swing open, revealing a small room with a huge bell in the center.

Hudson stepped into the room and instinctively touched the bell, then turned to Melody. "Does anyone ring it?"

With a sad little smile lingering at the corners of her mouth, Melody shook her head. "The pull mechanism for ringing the bell broke not long after the ministry started, and we didn't have the money to fix it. Even though we have more funds now, we use it for more important things."

"That's too bad." Hudson wondered whether someone on his crew could fix it free of charge. Would that make Melody smile? He'd like to see that.

Melody rubbed her hand along the curve of the bell. "It has a beautiful sound. I've been told that when this place was Upton College, they would ring the bell every hour. And they would ring it twenty-four times to call the students to chapel."

"I hope I can hear it sometime."

"That would be nice." Melody stepped toward the window on the other side of the room. "Come take a look at the view."

Hudson joined her at the small opening in the wall. From high above the quad, the walkways spreading out from the fountain looked like the spokes of a wheel. Even in the middle of winter when the trees had no leaves and the grass was pale green, the redbrick buildings with the white columns gave the campus a stately air. "This place must be beautiful in the spring."

"It is, and it's a wonderful place for a lot of people to get a new start with their lives and live out their final days. I'm so glad I work here."

Hudson got the feeling that everyone who worked here

loved the place. They treated each other like family. He wanted to be part of something like this. Conrick Industries had grown so big that people didn't know each other anymore. He'd like to make Conrick Construction a family-oriented place.

"You seem lost in thought."

Nodding, Hudson smiled at Melody. "Just thinking about the work ahead."

"Speaking of work, let's see that entrance."

As they made their way back through the chapel, Hudson stopped for a moment and looked at the stained-glass windows. "These are real works of art."

"They are a treasure we need to preserve."

Hudson's eye caught the inscription on the gold plate below one of the windows. "Wait." He walked closer and pointed to the plate. "See this?"

Melody came nearer. "A relative of yours?"

"In memory of Maisy Conrick. I believe she's some relation, but I'm not sure." Hudson rubbed a hand across his chin. "I'll ask my dad."

"One of your ancestors may have contributed money to the college at one time."

Hudson nodded. "They may have. That gives me a real connection here."

Melody looked up at him with a surprised expression. "I'm beginning to believe you are sentimental."

"I told you I am. Does that give me brownie points in your book?"

Melody gave him an annoyed glance. "I don't keep track of such things."

"Good to know." Even though she tried to put on an irritated act, Hudson wasn't buying it. Even today he was making inroads.

Melody hurried outside and around the side of the building. "That entrance is this way. It's seldom used, so I'm afraid there may be some undergrowth we'll need to remove."

"For sure. You've got a jungle back here with all this kudzu." Hudson pushed away the tangle of vines hanging from the trees along the rutted road. "And this road isn't in very good shape."

"The last time we used it was last October when we had a fire in one of the children's homes. I don't remember the last time before that."

"Was anyone hurt?"

"No, it was a lightning strike that caught the roof on fire, so everyone got out."

"Was there much damage?"

"Yeah, the roof collapsed."

"Wow! That must've been scary."

Melody released a harsh breath. "It was, but everyone came together, and it all worked out."

"Funny how that happens."

Melody stopped and stared at him. "No, not funny. God says all things work for good for those who love Him and are called according to His purpose."

Even though she said she didn't collect brownie points, his had just hit zero. All the goodwill he'd garnered over the past hour had sunk into one of the ruts in the road. "That's what I should've said."

Grimacing, Melody placed a hand over her heart. "I'm sorry. I didn't mean to come across as a pious know-it-all. I just know how so many good things came out of that fire and that God's hand was in it."

"I'd like to hear about them."

Melody slowed her pace as they traversed the uneven

road, then began to share. "We had to find places for everyone to stay, and that resulted in two brothers, Zach and Tyler, being housed with Adam Bailey. At the time, Brady was renting a room from Adam. That whole mix of folks resulted in Brady and Kirsten falling in love and deciding to adopt Zach and Tyler. They're getting married in the chapel in April, and the adoption will follow soon afterward. More kids got to move into the newly renovated house."

"You're right. God made good out of bad." Hudson took in Melody's joy as she talked about these wonderful things. Her happiness in serving God here made him more convinced that he'd done the right thing in going after the bid. He would make it work, even though their budget would be tight.

"It's wonderful to see God's hand in things that happen."

Hudson let Melody's elation over her work wash over him. Would his work here give him that kind of joy? Would she ever give him a chance to get to know her better, or would she hold him at arm's length forever?

They continued on the path until they came to the gate. Melody glanced over at him. "Will this entrance be big enough for your equipment?"

"It should be." Hudson put a hand on the top of the metal gate. "How does this work?"

"It's triggered with this siren-operated sensor for big fire engines that can't get through the front gate like ambulances and police cars can. That's why this one is rarely used."

"Since we don't have sirens, how can we use it?"

"I'll give you an access code, but I want you alone to

have it." She eyed him as if she was gauging his ability to keep the code to himself. "We can't be too careful. Ever."

"I understand, and I won't let you down." Hudson nodded. "Can you give me the dimensions of the vehicles that can go through the front gate?"

"I can't right now, but I'll get you that information."

"Good. I won't use this unless it is absolutely necessary." Hudson pushed himself away from the gate. "Thanks for the tour."

"You're welcome." She smiled up at him. "I enjoyed it."

Her smile made his heart race. He hated for their time together to end. "Do you have time for a cup of coffee?"

She didn't answer right away, just stared at him as if he'd ask her to skydive with him. Finally, she shook her head. "Sorry. I've got a meeting with one of my ladies this afternoon. We're going to The Village store to pick out some clothes for her job interview."

"Okay, maybe another time." Hudson held his breath as he waited for her response.

Melody shrugged. "We'll be too busy in the coming days. Coffee will have to wait."

"Sure." So she wasn't going to turn him down outright, but it seemed she would always find some excuse to avoid him. He reminded himself again that patience was his friend.

It was probably for the best. He'd pursued Nicole with abandon and she'd been all too willing. Melody's reluctance reminded him that he should take his time to get to know her. Although he'd still like a real date, working together would help him determine her sincerity.

They fell silent as they made their way back toward the quad. Melody loped ahead at her usual clip. Suddenly

her foot went down into one of the ruts, and she stumbled
forward. Before Hudson could grab her, she landed hard
on the dusty, gravel-covered ground. Her right shoe flew
into the air along with her purse.

He hurried to her side. "Are you okay?"

She didn't answer, her expression dazed. Then she
shook her head, her look turning to one of pain as she
rubbed her right ankle. "I did something to my ankle."

"Can you stand?" He placed a hand under one of her
elbows.

Melody nodded, but grimaced as he helped her up. "I
can't put any weight on my foot, and my poor shoe lost
its heel."

"Lean on me, and let's not worry about that." Hudson reached over and retrieved her purse and the shoe.
He held up the black pump, its heel hanging on by a thin
piece of leather. "No wonder you took a spill and twisted
your ankle. Let's hope it's not broken."

"How will I keep my appointment?" Misery painted
her face.

Hudson stuffed the shoe into his jacket pocket. "There's
only one way. I'll carry you."

Melody's eyes opened wide. "I can't let you do that."

"Sure you can."

"I'll call security. They'll come get me with the golf
cart." Glancing over at him, Melody stood on one leg
while she leaned on his arm. "My phone's in my purse.
Can you get it?"

"Okay." Still holding Melody up, Hudson reached into
her purse and retrieved her phone. "Here."

"Thanks." She immediately punched in a number.

Hudson listened to her one-sided conversation with
someone name Jeremy, who was obviously on his way

to rescue her. Hudson tried not to be disappointed that he couldn't be her knight in shining armor. Instead, his request to see the emergency entrance had caused all the trouble. "So security's on the way?"

Melody nodded as she continued to lean on him. "It should only take a few minutes for them to get here."

"Are you sure you're not getting tired of standing on one leg?"

"I'm okay. Really."

Before Hudson could make another comment, her cell phone rang. She glanced at it before accepting the call. "Jeremy? What's going on?"

Again Hudson listened while she talked, her face a picture of worry. "Okay. I'll be fine."

"What's wrong?" Hudson asked as soon as she ended the call.

She blew out a harsh breath. "The golf cart has stalled. Jeremy thinks the battery's dead."

Hudson studied her expression. Did he dare make his suggestion again? She didn't have much choice this time. No one else was coming to get her. "Guess you'll have to let me carry you if you want to go anywhere."

She gazed up at him, anxiety and pain painting her face. "Seems that way."

"Don't worry. I won't drop you."

She laughed halfheartedly. "Let's hope not."

"Put an arm around my neck, and then I'll pick you up." Hudson leaned over slightly and smiled. Maybe he would get to be her hero after all.

Melody held her breath as she put her arm around Hudson's neck. She hoped she wasn't too heavy. What a silly thought! He'd volunteered, so he'd better have a strong back. He put an arm under her legs at the knee and lifted her off the ground with apparent ease. She breathed a sigh of relief.

"Off we go." He grinned at her again. "Where do you want me to take you?"

"The nursing home, where I can get a wheelchair."

"Are you sure you don't want to go straight to my car so I can drive you to your doctor's office?"

"Let me talk to the nurses and see what they think."

As Hudson strode down the road toward the quad, Melody endeavored to concentrate on something other than how being in his strong arms made her pulse thunder. She didn't know which was worse. Her throbbing ankle or her racing heart. She tried not to think of either one, but she failed, especially when he looked down at her with that half smile that told her he had her right where he wanted her.

"You doing okay?"

She nodded, not trusting herself to speak. When Hudson was about halfway to the nursing home, the whirring sound of an electric golf cart reached her ears. She looked toward the sound. "Jeremy must've gotten the engine started again. He's headed our way. You can put me down."

"But I was having so much fun holding you in my arms."

Melody didn't know whether to laugh or be annoyed. "The fun can't last forever."

"Now you tell me." Hudson set Melody back on her feet, still supporting her by the elbow. "You can still lean on me until the cart arrives."

Melody looked up at him. Lean on him. She hated the thought of leaning on anyone. She wanted to depend on herself, not some man. Christopher had understood that about her. He'd loved her independence. Macho types like Hudson wanted to be a protector. Another thing to remember when she gazed into those maple-syrup eyes and let him tempt her to disregard her caution about men who took chances. "I'll be fine. Jeremy will be here in seconds."

"Suit yourself." Hudson released her elbow and stood there with his arms crossed.

As soon as he let go she tried to put weight on her sore ankle. It hurt, but she wouldn't let him see her grimace. "Good. Everything will be okay."

In less than a minute, Jeremy drove up beside her. "I'm here at your service. Do you need help getting in the cart?"

"No need to get out. I'll help her." Hudson waved Jeremy back, taking hold of her arm again and assisting her as she slid onto the padded seat.

Jeremy returned to his place behind the steering wheel. "I'm sorry about the delay. It did this to me the other day, too."

Melody leaned forward. "We need to get this taken care of. We don't want you to be without transportation."

"Will do. Where do you want to go?"

Hudson squeezed in beside her. "To the nursing home."

Melody tried not to let Hudson's interference bother her. She wanted to tell him she could speak for herself, but that would only make things worse.

As they drew closer to their destination, she spied Kirsten coming down the walk with a wheelchair. Melody glanced over at Hudson. "How did Kirsten know I needed that?"

"After we talked, I knew you would want one, so I sent her a text." Jeremy pulled to a stop at the end of the walk.

Kirsten hurried toward them. "What happened?"

After thanking Jeremy for his help, Melody explained everything as Hudson assisted her into the wheelchair. Invalid status didn't mesh with her plans. "Can you take a look at my ankle and tell me whether I need to see a doctor?"

"Of course." Kirsten pushed the wheelchair through the front door while Hudson held it open. Once inside, Kirsten hunkered down. "Does it hurt when I press here?"

"Yes."

"How about here?"

"Not so much." Melody shook her head. "But it's throbbing."

Kirsten straightened. "You appear to have a bad sprain. You don't have to go to the doctor right away, but you should rest. You can't be running all over campus in your usual manner."

"But what am I going to do about Amy? She's expecting me to help her pick out clothes for her interview." Melody let out a long sigh, knowing her day was a shambles.

"Is there someone you can call to help?" Kirsten asked.

Melody picked up her phone from her lap. "I'll call Debra McCoy, who volunteers at the shop."

Kirsten stepped closer. "Before you do anything else, listen to my instructions. Besides the rest, put ice on the ankle for twenty minutes and wrap it in a compression bandage. Then go home and elevate your foot. If things don't get better, then you'll need to see the doctor about an X-ray."

"Okay, but I have to make that phone call." The task

done, Melody looked up at Kirsten. "Debra said she'd help Amy and bring her back to campus if we get her over there."

"I'll give you both a ride." Hudson stepped forward.

Her pulse skittering, Melody glanced his way. Somehow she'd forgotten he was here. Or maybe she'd only tried to block his image from her mind. "Did your chauffer bring you in that limo?"

"Not today. I had to drive myself. I do that sometimes." Hudson gave her a wry smile.

Of course, multiple cars for the multimillionaire. Melody searched her mind for some way to decline his offer, but none came to mind. Once again, he had her right where he wanted her—in need of his services.

"That would be perfect," Kirsten replied before Melody could respond. "I'll be right back with that ice and bandage."

Melody sighed. "While you do that, I'll give Amy a call."

A little later, Melody sat sideways on the backseat of Hudson's SUV with her legs stretched out and an ice pack atop her well-wrapped ankle. A pair of crutches lay on the floor beside her. Amy sat in the front passenger seat and chatted comfortably with Hudson about her children and her job prospects. Melody wished she could feel as relaxed with the man. She wasn't sure why she was letting him tie her emotions in knots for absolutely no reason.

When they arrived at The Village store, Debra came out to meet them, poking her head into the SUV. "I'm so sorry to hear what happened, but I'll take good care of Amy. Don't worry about a thing."

"Thanks. I appreciate your help." Melody smiled.

Debra looked at Hudson. "You take good care of our Melody. She needs some pampering."

"Yes, ma'am. I sure will."

She refrained from rolling her eyes as Debra closed the door and she and Amy waved. Melody didn't need Hudson Conrick to pamper her. As he drove his SUV onto the main road, she chastised herself for the negative thoughts. He was being kind, and she should be thankful for his helpfulness. During the drive to her house, she prayed for a more charitable nature.

"How you doing back there?"

"I'm okay." Her ankle had quit throbbing. The ice had probably dulled the ache. "I forgot to ask if you remember how to get to my house."

"I certainly do. It's etched in my memory. It's fun being your chauffeur, but you don't have to call me James."

So he remembered her little story, but was he making fun of her? "Okay. Home, Hudson."

He laughed, and the sound made her heart lighter as she settled back for the ride. After he parked in the driveway, he opened the door for her and handed her the crutches.

"Thanks."

"Do you need some help? I can always carry you again."

"Thank you, but I'll be able to maneuver with the crutches. You can carry this." Melody handed him the ice pack.

"If you give me your keys, I can go ahead and open the door so you can walk right in."

"Good idea." She fished them from her purse, and while Hudson trotted off to open the door, Melody maneuvered out of the backseat, being careful not to put any weight on the tender ankle. She adjusted the crutches and made her way up the walk. When she reached the threshold, Hudson was there to give her an assist through the doorway. She didn't fight it. He was here to help, and she should let him.

"I'll stay right beside you in case you need support." He accompanied her into the living room.

Melody sat on the couch and swung her legs up, then looked over at him. "Thanks for your help. I should be okay now."

Staring at her, Hudson stood there with his arms crossed at his trim waist. "And I'm sticking around for a while to make sure of it."

"Really. I'm fine. There's no need for you to stay."

"Who's going to replenish your ice pack or get you a pillow to prop your leg on? If you don't keep it elevated, your ankle will swell even more."

Melody tried not to frown. She didn't want him hanging around. "Is this a ploy to get another date with me?"

Hudson shook his head. "I'm only here to make sure you have everything you need. I won't pester you for another date. You made it quite clear that you don't want to go out with me again. So I'll bow to your wishes, but if you ever change your mind, let me know."

"Okay." She'd gotten what she wanted. So why did a ping of disappointment sound in her mind and settle in her heart?

Hudson grinned at her. "You remember what you said about God using everything for good. He's going to make something out of this, too."

Melody gave him a helpless smile. "I had that coming."

"I wasn't trying to give you a hard time. I mean it."

"Okay. We'll see what He has prepared for me."

"And me." Hudson pulled his phone from his pocket. "I'm going to order you something to eat. What would you like?"

Melody shrugged, resigning herself to Hudson's presence. He wasn't after another date, so why did being with him bother her? "Whatever. I'm really not that hungry."

"You need to eat something. I'll order pizza. Pepperoni and mushroom?"

Closing her eyes, Melody nodded and laid her head back on the decorative pillow. Hudson liked her favorite kind of pizza. What did that say about him? She had to quit examining every little thing about him. Would admitting her fascination with him from the beginning help her deal with the attraction? She might as well. She couldn't deny it, and his constant presence in her life for the foreseeable future might require more resistance to his appeal than she could muster. At some point, would her heart overrule her head? Would her good sense succumb to the charms of a kind and attractive man even though he took chances that frightened her?

"You awake?" Hudson's whispered question made her eyes pop open.

"Yeah. I was resting as per instructions from Kirsten." Melody smiled, glad he couldn't read her thoughts. She gave herself a mental shake. The pain from her ankle and weariness from a sleepless night made her thinking fuzzy. She would get through today, and tomorrow she would find her fortitude again.

"You rest. Here's a pillow and a fresh ice pack." After she lifted her ailing ankle onto the pillow, he held up the ice pack. "Me or you? I don't want to put it in the wrong place and cause you more pain."

"Lay it down gently." His concern punched one more hole in her resistance.

After he placed the ice pack on her ankle, he looked down at her. "TV, book, music or quiet?"

Melody gazed up at him. Quiet was out of the question. Too much time to think about him. "You mean you don't want to talk to me?"

"We can talk." Hudson settled on the ottoman next to the couch, his long legs stretched out in front of him. "What do you want to talk about?"

She didn't know why she'd said that. Fuzzy brain again. What on earth did she have to say to Hudson Conrick? Nothing. Did they have anything in common besides liking the same kind of pizza? The pizza couldn't get here fast enough. Sighing, she shrugged. "On second thought, I'm too tired to talk."

"I understand. You rest. I've got work I can do." Still sitting on the ottoman, he pulled out his cell phone and began tapping the screen. "And I'd better call Ian and let him know why I didn't show up for our discussion about the Valentine banquet."

Nodding, Melody closed her eyes again, but images of Hudson still cluttered her mind. She wanted to think about anything else, but her thoughts kept coming back to the handsome man a few feet away. She kept drifting in and out of sleep, dreams of Hudson filling her subconscious. In her dreams, he was kissing her. Which was more troubling? The dreams about the man or the reality of him sitting in her living room?

Chapter Five

The doorbell rang, but it didn't seem to faze Melody. She continued to sleep. Hudson cast another look at her over his shoulder as he went to answer the door. After paying for the pizza, he carried the box into the living room and set it on the ottoman. He stared down at Melody, her blond hair falling across the pillow as she slept. Her beauty captured his heart. But it was more than her appearance that captivated him. It was her spirit.

Although she didn't seem to care much for him, she cared about all the folks at The Village. He'd meant what he'd said when he'd told her he wouldn't press for another date, but he hoped their association over the next few months would soften her attitude toward him.

Hudson touched her arm. "Melody, the pizza's here."

Her eyes blinked open, and she stared at him. She blinked again and put a hand over her heart. "Oh, I'm so sorry. I didn't mean to doze off, but I didn't sleep well last night. I guess it caught up to me."

Hudson smiled, his heart thudding as she looked up at him with those light brown eyes. "That's okay. I got lots of work done, and you got the rest you needed."

"What time is it?"

"It's nearly six." Hudson opened the pizza box. "Are you hungry now?"

Melody tried to sit up. "A little."

"How's the ankle?"

"Better." She looked over at him. "Have you been putting the ice pack on and off?"

"I have." He smiled again, his heart still thundering. "I make a good nurse."

She laughed. "Kirsten will be impressed."

"I'll get some plates. And what can I get you to drink?"

"I don't expect you to wait on me."

"That's why I'm here. Rest. Remember, that's what Kirsten said. Stay off that ankle."

"I've been doing plenty of resting."

"More can't hurt, and as long as I'm here, you might as well take advantage of my assistance."

Melody sighed. "Okay. I'll take a cola. Lots of ice."

Hudson made his way into the kitchen and flipped on the light. Melody's kitchen was a clear reflection of her. Neat—with everything in place. He suspected he could eat off her floors. He found the plates, glasses, flatware and napkins. Minutes later he returned to the living room. He handed her the cola. "Here you go."

She sat up with her leg propped up on the ottoman. "Thanks. There are coasters in the drawer of the end table."

Hudson got out two coasters, then served the pizza before taking a seat on the chair that sat at an angle to the couch. "Would you like me to give thanks?"

"Sure."

"Lord, thank You for Melody and her service to those who are in need. Please heal her ankle quickly so she can be back at work in full force. We thank You for this food. In Jesus's name. Amen."

"Thank you. I appreciate your prayer." Melody stared at him, a twinkle of appreciation in her eyes.

Maybe he'd just picked up a few brownie points. With the silly thought running through his mind he took a bite of pizza. He wasn't back in grade school trying to impress his teacher, but he wanted to be on Melody's good side. He wanted to get to know her better, but she kept her feelings close to her chest—except for her wish not to go out with him again.

He shouldn't care. He'd told her he wasn't going to ask her for another date. So why did he keep thinking about it? Was he already regretting it? Was it something that would come back to bite him? Maybe her rejection was crushing his ego, and he couldn't dismiss the challenge of changing her mind.

"How's the pizza?"

"Good. I was hungrier than I thought." She took a bite.

"Glad you're enjoying it."

"Thanks for your help."

"You're welcome, and I believe you'll need my help again tomorrow."

A little pucker formed between her eyebrows. "Why?"

"Your car's still at The Village, and you'll need a ride in the morning."

"Oh, yeah, but you don't need to worry about it." She waved a hand at him. "I'll get someone from The Village to help me. You don't need to go out of your way."

"It's not out of my way when I'll be headed there to oversee the beginning of the construction project."

"You're starting already?"

"We're going to bring in materials tomorrow."

"But I haven't given you the dimensions of the front entrance."

Hudson shook his head. "We're only bringing in smaller equipment, so we'll be ready when the permits are in place."

"Isn't it out of the way for you?"

"No. I drive right by here, and even if I wasn't going to be there for the construction project, I still have an appointment with Ian." Hudson smiled despite the fact that she wasn't eager to accept his help.

"Oh. Okay. I guess I'd be silly not to accept your generous offer." Her shoulders slumped as she took another bite of pizza.

"Will you be able to drive your car tomorrow?"

Melody set down her slice of pizza. "I think so. I'll take it easy tonight, and I'll be a new woman in the morning."

"I hope not too new. I kind of like the woman you are." Except the part that wouldn't go on another date with him.

"You do?" Her eyes grew wide.

"Why do you seem so surprised that I like you?"

She appeared to be weighing his question, her eyes focused on something across the room. When she looked back at him, she wore a doubtful expression. "You're only trying to get on my good side."

"Of course I am." Hudson grinned. "You're the boss lady, and I wouldn't want to displease you."

"You really are trying to chalk up brownie points."

"I freely admit that I am, but I was being completely serious. I admire what you're doing at The Village. In fact, I mentioned your work to my mother, and she's going to call you about talking to one of her women's groups."

Again she seemed hesitant to speak. "I'm always happy to share the work we do."

"Good."

Melody finished her slice of pizza and leaned back on the couch while she took a sip of her drink. She seemed lost in thought, and Hudson got the feeling that she wasn't up for more conversation.

After they ate, he took the plates and glasses to the kitchen and put them in the nearly empty dishwasher. He put the leftover pizza in the refrigerator, then came back to the living room. Melody had returned to her reclining position with her leg propped up on the pillow at the end of the couch.

"If you think you'll be okay, I'm headed home. If you need anything, you can call me."

He hated for the evening to end, but he didn't want to overstay his welcome.

She looked up at him. "You know bringing me home would've been enough, but thank you for staying and serving me supper."

"You're welcome."

"What time can I expect you in the morning?"

"Is quarter till eight too early?"

"No, I'll be ready." She gave him a little wave, something sad in her expression. "I'd see you to the door, but I'm a little incapacitated."

"Good night. I'll see myself out." Hudson closed her front door, her soft farewell still echoing in his ears.

He walked to his vehicle while he replayed the evening in his mind. They'd shared a good time, and any doubts of her sincerity were rapidly receding. Was he right to conclude that she wasn't another Nicole with ulterior motives?

* * *

The next morning Hudson wasn't even out of his SUV before Melody was swinging down her walk on those crutches. She could even be speedy with those. He hurried around to the passenger side to open the door. "Good morning. You're getting along very well with those things. What did you do? Practice with them after I left last night?"

She laughed as he helped her into the car. "No, they're not that hard to use. I'm not an invalid, you know."

"I know that for sure." Hudson put the crutches in the back, then hopped into the driver's seat. "I'm ready to get this project started, and I'm thankful for another sunny day, despite the cool temperature. February has started out colder than January this year."

"I hope for the best and live for spring." Laughing, she buckled her seat belt.

When they arrived at The Village, Hudson drove his SUV as close to the administration building as he could so Melody wouldn't have to walk very far. He retrieved her crutches from the backseat and brought them around to her. "You know you could've called Jeremy to drive you right up to the door."

"He's got his rounds to make, and I wouldn't want to disrupt his schedule. Besides, I can get where I want to go quite easily. Another day, and I won't even have to use these things."

"Don't start putting weight on that ankle before it's ready."

She frowned at him. "Are you a doctor now?"

"No, I just know about sprained ankles. I've had a few. Take it easy." He waved as Melody disappeared through the side door.

After Hudson parked in the nearest lot, he meandered back toward the administration building for his meeting with Ian. As he approached the reception area, he noticed Lovie was busy typing something, the keys clicking as her fingers flew over the keyboard. He stopped for a moment in front of the desk. "Good morning, Lovie."

She glanced up, a smile forming on her lips. "Just the man I wanted to see."

Hudson knit his eyebrows. "Why?"

"Because I just figured out why I know your name."

Hudson's radar went up. Did she know his family or the family business? "How's that?"

"I heard Mr. Ian talking about you and Ms. Melody. You were the one who took her to the fund-raiser." Lovie shook a finger at him. "You two make a pretty good pair. And I have a marvelous record on knowing when people match up well. So you two are next on my list."

Hudson's laughter echoed in the reception area. "This could be interesting. Does Melody know about your list?"

"She knows, but she doesn't know I've finally put her on it and paired her with you."

Hudson laughed again. "So what does being on this list of yours mean?"

"That you'll be the next bride and groom here at The Village."

Not sure how to respond, Hudson rolled that information around in his mind. Melody fascinated him, and he wanted to get to know her better, go out on a few more dates, but marriage? That was a leap. Eyeing Lovie, he shook his head. "That's getting a little ahead of where I'm at."

Lovie nodded. "I know, but you'll eventually come around, and so will Ms. Melody. I've got you two in my sights."

"Then, maybe I'd better stay out of range."

Chuckling, Lovie shook her head. "Once you get there, you can't get out of range. Just saying."

"Guess we'll see what happens." Shaking his head again, he headed toward Ian's office. "Take care, and don't do too much matchmaking."

"Never too much." Her laughter followed Hudson as he turned the corner.

He knocked on Ian's door and hoped this upcoming conversation would give him the information he needed.

"Come on in." Ian clapped Hudson on the back. "Congratulations again on winning the bid to complete our women's shelter expansion."

Hudson smiled. "Yeah, the work's beginning as we speak. I'm out here to make sure we get things moving. And to find out where you can use me for the Valentine banquet, since we never discussed it after Melody twisted her ankle."

"Yeah, that's been rough on her. As soon as you told me about her accident, I knew it would cramp her style." Ian chuckled. "It's killing her, but I told her it was a chance to stop and smell the roses."

"You've talked to her already this morning?"

"Yeah. Why?"

"Because I just dropped her off, and she didn't look very slow to me."

Curiosity flashed across Ian's expression. "You drove her over?"

"I did. I gave her a ride home after she got her ankle wrapped, too. I ordered her a pizza and played nursemaid until I had worn out my welcome." Hudson didn't miss the surprise that wiped out Ian's curious look.

"Interesting. Is something going on that I should know about?"

Hudson wondered what he should tell Ian. After all, he'd arranged their blind date, but that was about the fund-raising, not romance. "Even if something is, I'm not sure you should know about it."

Shaking his head, Ian let out a halfhearted laugh. "Are you telling me to mind my own business?"

"Not really. There isn't anything to tell."

"Would you like there to be?"

"Good question." Hudson shrugged. "Let's talk about the Valentine banquet, then we can discuss Melody and sponsoring the fountain."

"What's the occasion?"

"I'm not sure yet."

Ian nodded and motioned toward the black leather chairs in front of his desk. "I was surprised when Adam invited you to participate, but I think he has his reasons."

"What would those be?"

"It might have to do with one Melody Hammond. She seems to be the topic of the hour." A slow smile crossed Ian's face. "I think Adam's trying to do a little matchmaking."

"Him, too?"

Ian chuckled. "Maybe. The matchmaking bug seems to be contagious around this place."

Hudson joined the laughter. "I've met Lovie, and she already has me on her list. Do you suppose she shared her list with Adam?"

"Wouldn't surprise me."

Hudson nodded and changed the subject. "So what am I doing for this banquet?"

"How's your skill in the kitchen?"

"As in cooking?" Hudson raised his eyebrows.

"No, preparing the plates."

"Sounds like something I can handle."

"Then, that'll be your assignment."

"Now I'd like to discuss the fountain."

Ian eyed him. "Does this have anything to do with Melody?"

"It does." Hudson held his breath as he waited for Ian's reaction.

"If you were thinking of Valentine's Day, that day's been taken for months."

"I'm not interested in Valentine's Day." Hudson rested his elbows on the armrests. "I don't have a specific day picked out yet. But I also have another idea I want to run by you before I do the fountain."

"Sure. What's on your mind?"

"Before Melody sprained her ankle, she took me up in the bell tower of the chapel and told me that the bell can't be rung anymore because the mechanism is broken. I'd like to have our company fix—"

"We've decided not to fix it because we can make better use of our money."

"Hear me out before you dismiss the idea. There'll be no charge to you. I'm paying for it as a gift to The Village. I'd like this to be a surprise, and I want to sponsor the fountain on the day the bell is ready to ring."

Ian sat back in his chair and laced his fingers behind his head as he raised his eyebrows. "So you want to surprise Melody?"

Hudson wished he could explain his thoughts about her, but he wasn't sure of them himself. "Yes, and I want to get to know her better."

"Then, take her out again."

Frowning, Hudson sighed. If he wanted to talk about Melody, he would have to admit that she wouldn't go out with him again. "I know she had a good time with me at the fund-raiser, and we had an enjoyable evening last night, but she won't go on another date with me."

"Did she say why?"

"Yeah, she says we come from different worlds. I like to live on the edge and she likes to play it safe. And the two don't mix."

Ian shrugged. "She could be right. She has a good reason."

"What?"

"First, her father died in a plane crash when she was young. Then three years ago her fiancé was killed by a roadside bomb while he was delivering aid to people in Afghanistan. She begged him not to go because of the danger, but he went anyway because he wanted to help."

The air sucked out of Hudson's lungs. No wonder she'd turned pale when he'd mentioned stepping into a mine-field during the dinner dance. "That's tough. Are you saying she's never gotten over the death of her fiancé?"

"She doesn't talk about it. Everyone believes she throws herself into her work so she doesn't have to think about it." Ian shook his head. "For a long time, no one could convince her to go on a date at all, but lately, she's agreed to some. You were one of them."

"Have any of the others resulted in a second?"

"Not that I know of, but I'm not the dating coordinator around here." Ian chuckled. "Ask Annie about that."

Hudson scooted forward in his seat. "But didn't you arrange my night with her?"

"I mentioned you to Annie, and she took over." Ian got up and walked over to the window and made a sweeping gesture toward the view of the quad outside. "Melody is interested in only one thing—her work here."

Joining Ian at the window, Hudson contemplated the new information about Melody's fiancé. Add that to the deaths of her brother and father, and Hudson could see why she wanted to stay away from men who took chances on anything. And he wasn't willing to give up his adventures for a woman he didn't know all that well, even though she fascinated him. "So you're saying my chances of getting a second date are slim?"

Ian nodded. "I would venture to say almost impossible."

"Thanks for the ego boost and encouragement."

"Always glad to be of service." Ian chuckled.

"Could I ask you a personal question?"

Smiling wryly, Ian leaned against the windowsill. "That all depends."

Hudson shook his head. "I know that's a loaded question. Let me ask it, and if you don't want to answer, feel free to ignore it."

"Okay."

"Am I remembering correctly that you were divorced while we were in law school?" Hudson watched for signs that he might have offended Ian.

Ian looked out the window again as if he was trying to find an answer. "Yeah, Annie and I divorced while I was in law school."

Hudson smiled. He'd always loved happy endings— maybe the result of growing up with three older sisters. "So you remarried?"

Ian lowered his gaze, then looked back at Hudson. "Yeah. We're both in recovery for substance abuse. We had a lot of forgiving to do, but with God's help we're going to do it right this time."

Ian went on to tell Hudson about their reconciliation and remarriage after Annie had come to The Village for help in regaining custody of her daughter and son. No wonder Melody hadn't wanted to discuss the details and had suggested that he ask Ian about it.

Hudson clapped Ian on the back. "Hey, thanks for explaining everything. I'm glad things worked out for you and Annie."

"Yeah, me, too." Ian nodded.

"Will Melody be hands-on with the women's shelter project?"

Ian smiled. "Are you hoping she is?"

"I thought maybe if—"

"If you're around her enough, she'll warm up to your reckless ways?"

Hudson shook his head. "I'm not sure I know what I'm hoping for. Maybe just a chance."

"Well, she and Adam are the ones keeping track of the new construction, so you'll probably see a lot of her. On the other hand, she's one busy woman with a lot of irons in the fire. No telling how much time she'll spend there." Ian gave Hudson a curious look. "Even after you helped Melody with her sprained ankle, she's giving you the cold shoulder?"

Hudson laughed halfheartedly. "I'd say it's lukewarm."

Ian clapped Hudson on the back. "Hudson, you're my friend, but I'm also Melody's friend, and I'm warning you to tread lightly with her. I'd like to see her find someone who can make her happy. She's not a woman you can take out a few times and toss aside. She's been through a lot of tragedy, and she has a tender heart. I won't stand by and let you hurt her."

Hudson didn't know what to make of his friend's warning. How was he supposed to know whether to pursue a serious relationship with her unless they went out again—got to know each other better? "I have no intention of hurting her."

"I know you wouldn't mean to, but I remembered how you operated when we were in law school. You went through women faster than you went through legal pads." Ian gave him a cautionary look. "You can't do that with Melody."

Hudson took a deep breath, remembering the way he'd tried to bury his hurt over Nicole. "I'm not the same guy you knew in law school. Being in the army gave me a different perspective about life. And in my defense, most of those women I dated back then were more interested in my bank account than they were in me."

Ian nodded. "I'll give you that, but I wanted you to know you can't toy with Melody's heart."

"She won't go out with me anyway, so maybe it's a moot point."

"You know." Smiling, Ian rubbed a hand over his jawline. "We're having a Super Bowl party, and Melody will be there. You're welcome to come. Then you can get to know some of our group better, and maybe Melody will see you in a different light."

"Thanks for the invitation. I'll be there." Hudson extended his hand to Ian. "Thanks for seeing me, and I won't forget what you've told me. Now I'll let you get back to the important stuff."

"Reconnecting with an old friend is always important." Ian shook Hudson's hand.

Hudson walked into the hallway and stood there a moment, trying to resist the urge to knock on Melody's door. For now, he had to be satisfied that he'd seen her this morning on the drive over. Now he had to get to work.

While Hudson walked across the quad to the construction site, he thought about his conversation with Ian and Lovie. People everywhere were trying to tell him what to do and how to act. Did he appear directionless to those around him? Was that why his father had planned to run his life?

Hudson glanced over at the chapel and remembered Melody's invitation to attend church there. Did God have a plan for him? Hudson wanted to break away from the family business and not have to answer to his father for everything. He hadn't considered that his ideas might not be God's chosen path.

Although he'd gone to church with his family whenever he was home because his father had expected it, Hudson had to admit his faith wasn't what it should be. He'd pretty much drifted through the whole church thing. Had he come in contact with Ian again for a reason? How did a person know God's will for his life?

Hudson shook the questions away. He had his own vision for where he wanted to be and what he wanted to do, and he was sticking to it.

Chapter Six

The sight of the red Ferrari parked in front of Ian and Annie's house jumbled Melody's insides. There was only one person that car could belong to. How had she guessed that Hudson was a Ferrari? She should have known he'd be in the mix when Annie had invited her over for a Super Bowl party, something she wasn't that excited about.

A little get-together with a few friends. Were Ian and Annie trying to act as matchmakers?

Melody wondered how she should deal with Hudson. Why was he pursuing a poor girl from rural Georgia? Maybe she was a challenge he couldn't resist. If she fell all over him, would he turn and run the other way as fast as he could? If she put that plan into action and it didn't work, she could be in big trouble.

Even though he'd told her that he wasn't going to ask her for another date, his presence always put her on edge. He seemed to be around every corner on The Village campus—at the construction site, the administration building or at the cafeteria. His appeal had her running scared. She'd even considered packing her lunch and eating in her office, but she refused to let any man intimidate her into hiding.

She couldn't forget that in their interactions he'd been masquerading as a sedan with his down-home stories and good-old-boy persona, but in truth he was a sports car. There was only one thing she could do. She had to manufacture a smile and make the best of the evening. It couldn't be all bad with other people to act as a buffer between Hudson and her.

Melody took a deep breath as she made her way to the front door. She was thankful to have hung up her crutches a few days ago. Although she could feel a twinge of pain once in a while and she had to wear flats instead of heels, her ankle was nearly as good as new. Every time she felt a small ache, she thought of Hudson and the way he'd insisted on helping her that day. She didn't want to think nice things about him because they undermined her resistance.

She rang the doorbell. Annie opened the door. "Melody, come in." Annie leaned a little closer. "Hudson's here."

"Yeah, I figured that when I saw the Ferrari. Not too many of our acquaintances own one of those."

Annie laughed as she hung Melody's jacket in the coat closet. "Everyone's in the den. While we're waiting for the game to start, Hudson's entertaining us with some video."

Melody's nervousness increased but she tried to pretend he was any other guy, not someone who put her heart on a racetrack like one of his cars. She had to be friendly, but not too friendly. Walking a tightrope of emotions wouldn't make for a great evening.

When Melody entered the room, everyone was gathered around Hudson. Just as Annie had said, they were looking at something on the tablet he was holding. As she watched him, her heart bumped against her rib cage. If it could be possible, he was more handsome in a pair of blue jeans and a blue-and-white-plaid shirt than he was in a tuxedo or even the khakis and dress shirts he wore when he came to the campus.

"Hey, everyone, Melody's here." Annie propelled Melody toward the group.

Hudson looked up from the iPad. His intense scrutiny sent her heart into overdrive. She could handle this. No need to let his presence tie her in knots.

Melody smiled as she raised her hand halfway and gave a little wave. "What are y'all looking at?"

Kirsten pulled her into the group. "You've got to see this. Hudson skydives. So cool."

Melody tried to smile at Kirsten, who obviously had no idea that Melody wasn't excited about Hudson's skydiving or even the fact that he was here. "I'm not a fan."

Brady came up and put his arm around his fiancée's shoulders as he looked at Melody. "You'd think Kirsten would say the same thing since she's the woman who doesn't like to ride on cable cars dangling above the ground, but here she is saying how cool skydiving is."

Kirsten gave him an irritated look. "I've never known anyone who has actually jumped from a plane. I didn't say I was going to skydive. Hot-air balloon rides are as adventuresome as I want to get."

"I'm not sure I'd even like a balloon ride." Melody grimaced.

"Maybe you should see for yourself what we're talking about." Hudson grinned as he held out the iPad. "Take a look."

"Okay." Melody figured everyone would think she was unsociable if she didn't. She watched the video of Hudson jumping out of a plane, his parachute opening in a colorful display. After soaring over the forested hills in the Atlanta area, he made a pinpoint landing in an open field. She wanted to ask how he did it, but she decided not to engage him in conversation. He had enough attention from the others. Was she the only one who found the idea completely horrifying?

Closing the cover on the tablet, Hudson looked at her. "So was it as bad as you thought?"

Melody raised her eyebrows. "You really don't want me to answer that question."

Hudson pressed his lips together in a grim line. "So I didn't change your mind?"

"I'd rather not talk about it. The thought of it turns my stomach." Melody tried to smile to take the edge off her statement. "Let's discuss something else."

"Sure." He gave her a pointed look. "Did my mother call you about talking to her ladies' group?"

"She did, and she's set up a luncheon at her home." Melody stared back, wondering why Hudson was so interested in her project beyond the construction. Was he still trying to win the brownie points he'd joked about the day she'd sprained her ankle? She shouldn't doubt his sincerity. Was her attitude the result of fear—fear of letting this handsome, danger-loving man get too close?

"I'm sure that made her happy. She loves those kinds of events."

"Thanks for mentioning The Village to her. I always appreciate an opportunity to share the work we do." Melody hoped she sounded sincere. She really did love sharing the ministry, though standing up in front of a group of wealthy women wasn't something she was looking forward to. It was her least favorite part of the job.

"I have another fund-raising idea that I mentioned to Ian this evening. He seemed to like it, so I thought I'd run it by you." Hudson picked up the tablet from the end table and scrolled through the screen as he studied it. He held up the device for her to take a look. "Have you ever heard of a road-rally fund-raiser?"

Melody shook her head as she looked at the screen. "What is it?"

"Folks pay a fee to drive their cars along a predetermined route with clues that guide them to the end point. The team car coming closest to the course time set by the sponsors wins a prize. It's something an individual or a whole family can do." Hudson handed her the tablet. "You can read about it more in depth here."

Melody took it, her heart pounding at the thought of racing cars. How could that be a family event? She tried to focus on the screen, but the words swam before her eyes. She took a deep breath and let it out slowly as the words became clear. As she read, her fears began to subside.

Melody stared up at him, but before she could respond, Travis Hoffman, Kirsten Bailey's friend who had recently moved to Atlanta, approached.

"Melody, I wanted to congratulate you on the great fund-raiser." Travis smiled.

"Thanks, Travis." Why didn't he interest her? He fit the sedan model. Maybe that was the problem. Her head said "sedan," but her heart told her to go for the sports car. "Have you met Hudson?"

"Yes, we were talking about cars before you arrived." Travis motioned toward the front of the house. "I admit to being envious of his vehicle out there."

"We should find a time to do some racing." Hudson nodded. "If I set something up, would you participate?"

"Sure. That's something I've always wanted to do."

Oh, great! Hudson was going to get all these guys racing cars, even Travis, who didn't seem the type.

"Has Hudson told you about his road-rally idea?"

Travis shook his head as he looked over at Hudson. "I did one of those when I was in college for our fraternity. Are you doing one to raise money for The Village?"

"That's the thought." Hudson pointed to the tablet. "I was showing Melody what they're all about."

"That would be fun," Travis said.

"What do you think, Melody?" Hudson asked. "I'd help you set it up."

Melody tried to smile. That would mean another meeting with Hudson. Was he doing this on purpose? He wouldn't ask her for another date, but he would find every opportunity to be in each other's company. "I'll think about."

"Talk to Ian." Hudson nodded toward the other side of the room. "He's on board."

"I will." Melody wanted to get away. Could she escape now that Travis was here? "I'll see if Annie needs help in the kitchen and let you guys talk about cars or football or whatever."

"Yeah, the game will be starting soon. You don't want to miss the kickoff." Hudson's expression told Melody that he knew she was running away, but he didn't try to stop her. As she hurried across the room, she could hear the guys start their plans for a race. Maybe she should cut Hudson some slack. After all, Travis seemed interested in cars, too.

Did all men like to live on the edge or just certain

men? Christopher hadn't been one to live like that. He'd only wanted to help people in need. Why had God allowed Christopher to die? She didn't have the answer. She had to quit thinking about it or the negativity would ruin her evening.

Melody found Annie working in the kitchen. "Need some help?"

Her friend lifted a lid and stirred something in a big pot. "You should be spending time with Hudson."

"Was it your idea to invite him?"

"I don't remember. Ian and I made the guest list together." Annie shrugged and stirred some more. "Why?"

Melody frowned. "So I can tell you to stop pushing us together."

"What do you have against him?"

Melody let the question rattle around in her mind. Could she explain her reservations? The man had endeared himself to everyone here and at The Village. "Nothing. He's not my type."

"What's not to like about a handsome rich guy?"

Melody shrugged. "Do we have to discuss him?"

Annie raised her eyebrows as she gave Melody a skeptical look. "So he really is your type. You just don't want to admit it."

Melody huffed. "There's nothing to admit. You're trying to make something out of nothing."

"I remember when you were giving me advice about Ian, and I wasn't sure I wanted to listen—"

"But that was different. You and Ian had a history. I've only known Hudson for a few weeks, and we don't have much in common."

"Kirsten told me that was how Brady felt when they met. Look at what happened with them."

Melody pressed her lips together as she contemplated an argument to refute Annie's reasoning. "You don't understand."

"Then, explain it." Annie opened the oven and extracted a casserole dish and set it on a trivet.

"Another time. Is that your delicious buffalo chicken dip?"

"Well, it's Ian's mom's recipe." Annie chuckled. "She supplied me with most of the instructions for tonight's dishes."

"Can I help you serve the food?"

"You can, but that doesn't mean you'll get out of telling me why you're not interested in Hudson." Annie took off the oven mitts and laid them on the counter.

"I can try."

"But you won't succeed." Annie grinned as she handed Melody a bag of chips and a jar of salsa. "You can replenish the snacks in the den. I'm going to put some of the stuff on the breakfast bar and leave the rest in here."

Welcoming the diversion, Melody hurried to replenish the bowls on the coffee table. She glanced up at the TV. The game was already in progress. Folks had found seats on the sofa, on chairs or on the floor. She surveyed the room and spied Hudson standing near the breakfast bar, where Annie was putting more food.

He motioned to the empty bar stool next to him. "You can sit here, and I'll keep you company."

Waving the empty chip bag in the air, she made a move toward the kitchen. "I have to throw this away and put away the salsa jar."

"Go ahead. I'll be waiting for you to come back. We should discuss the road rally."

"I thought you were here to watch the game."

"I am, but I can do both." He gave her a wry smile.

Melody couldn't think of a good reason not to accept his invitation. Despite her earlier skepticism about the event, the idea had merit. "Okay."

"I'm looking forward to it." He turned his attention to the game.

How long could she hide out in the kitchen? Melody shook the question away. She had to learn to live with Hudson's presence. She'd already told herself that, but she wasn't doing a very good job. His kindness made her vulnerable to him.

When she returned, the game was still scoreless. People all around her cheered or moaned depending on how their chosen team was doing. Melody perched on the stool next to the one Hudson occupied.

"Welcome back."

Melody frowned. "I wasn't gone that long."

"Seemed like it."

Melody stared at him. What did he mean by that statement? She wasn't going to ask. She turned her attention to the game.

"Is your ankle still doing okay?"

Melody looked down at her foot. "Yeah. Didn't you ask me that this morning at church?"

He gave her a little smirk. "I did, but I'll keep asking until I see you wearing those heels again."

Melody held out her legs. "I hardly think I should be wearing heels with jeans."

"I've seen it done, and I had no idea you weren't a jeans-and-heels woman." He tapped the side of his head. "I'll sock that information away for future reference."

"And why would you need to do that?"

"Because I'm learning all about you. I like to know

as much about the people I work with as I can. It makes for good business."

"I suppose it does." Melody stared at him. Was he playing games with her, making her wonder whether his references were really about business? Annoyed with herself for even entertaining the idea that it might not be, she turned her attention to the game.

"Do you have a team?"

"No."

"Me, neither. I'd just like to see a good game." He gave her a sideways glance. "Are you one of those women who is only interested in the commercials?"

Melody shrugged. "I'm not that interested in this because Atlanta isn't playing. My brothers played football in high school, so I know a little about the game. And of course, I always cheered for the Dawgs when I was at Georgia."

"And I always cheered for the Gators."

Melody raised her eyebrows. "You went to the University of Florida?"

"I did."

"Did you play football?"

"And hurt this pretty face?" Hudson waved a hand in front of himself.

Melody laughed. "A guy who jumps out of planes and races cars is afraid of hurting his face?"

Hudson joined her laughter. "Just kidding. I was a slow bloomer. I was a puny kid growing up—all the way through high school. That's why I was taking dance lessons instead of playing football or basketball. I ran track so the guys chasing me weren't going to tackle me. For years my sisters were not only older than me but bigger than me, too. I finally had a growth spurt in college. I was excited to nearly top out at six feet."

A big roar filled the room, and several people jumped out of their seats, arms raised. One of the teams had scored, and Melody realized neither she nor Hudson had been paying attention. They'd been lost in their own conversation—a conversation she'd been enjoying too much for her own good. "Guess we'd better start watching the game."

"I was having more fun talking with you."

As a commercial played, a collective chuckle rolled through the room. Thankful for the distraction, Melody ignored Hudson's statement. She didn't want to make anything more of it than she should. She needed to get away before his banter sucked her in more than it already had. She slid off the stool and looked at him. "I'm going to load up a plate with bad-for-me food and mingle a little."

"So does that mean we won't be able to discuss the road rally?"

"We should leave that for another time."

"Tomorrow morning?"

Melody didn't relish the prospect, but she couldn't pass up anything that would raise money for The Village. "Sure. Stop by my office when you get to campus."

"I'll be there at eight."

During the rest of the game, Melody managed to keep her distance from Hudson, but from time to time she glanced in his direction and found him looking at her without a hint of apology. He didn't seem to mind that he'd been caught staring. She didn't want to think about him, but he seemed to find his way into her vision even when she wasn't looking his way.

She couldn't help thinking about him helping with the senior center Valentine's Day party. It was held the day before, and Melanie wondered if Hudson would have special plans for the actual holiday. Was there a rich debutante waiting in the wings for him? Why did that thought bother her? Her conflicting emotions about him left her unsettled. Why did she have to be attracted to a man who lived to do dangerous things? She couldn't deny the pull, but she intended to fight it.

But it was no use. By the time the evening was over, she had a throbbing headache from thinking about Hudson Conrick and her increasing feelings for him. He was just another man who liked to live on the edge. Even her dad, who'd flown cargo planes, had lived that way, refusing to listen to those who had advised him not to fly because of bad weather. He'd rolled the dice and died at the age of thirty-eight, leaving behind a young widow and four children. She didn't want to have an interest in a man who gambled with life…no matter how appealing.

The next morning Melody sat in her office while she waited for Hudson's promised visit. She tried to tell herself that she wasn't looking forward to their meeting or that she hadn't taken special care with her clothes, hair and makeup this morning. As the minute hand on the wall clock ticked toward eight thirty, Melody started to worry. Hudson was always prompt. Why was he late? Had he forgotten?

She picked up her phone from the desk and stared at it. Should she call him? With a deep sigh, she put the phone down. No. She would go on with her morning as planned. She turned to her computer screen and began to type reports.

When her phone rang, she grabbed it. Her heart pounded as she stared at the screen. Hudson. "Hey, is everything all right?"

"No. Got a real problem. Carter's been in a bad accident. I'm here at the hospital."

Melody's heart jumped into her throat. "How is he?"

"Don't know for sure. Docs are working on him now."

"Oh, Hudson, I'm so sorry. Is there anything I or anyone can do?"

"Yeah. His wife is here with her two toddlers, and they're a handful. Do you suppose you could come get them and take them over to their sitter's house?"

"I don't have car seats."

There was a momentary silence, and Melody wondered what was happening.

"Melody?" Hudson's voice sounded over the phone. "That's okay. You can use Tiffany's car after you get here."

"Are you at the local hospital?"

"Yeah."

"Where will I find you?"

"I'll meet you at the emergency entrance."

"Okay, I'll be there in a few minutes."

"Thanks."

Melody poked her head into Adam's office and let him know what had happened. Then she raced to her car. While she drove, she couldn't help reliving the day her brother had been taken to the hospital after his accident. Why did bad things happen to good people? Melody's pulse pounded in her head as she turned onto the main road.

During the trip, she prayed for Carter and tried to calm her own nerves. She wouldn't help anyone if she was in a panic. After she parked her car, she sprinted to the emergency entrance. She slowed her pace when she felt a twinge in her ankle. As she drew nearer, she spied Hudson standing just inside the sliding glass doors.

When she was only a foot away, he stepped outside. "Thanks for coming."

"Do you know anything more?"

He shook his head. "We won't know anything until they bring him out of surgery. Come this way, and I'll introduce you to Tiffany and the kids."

Melody had no idea how she could comfort Carter's wife. She wanted to give reassurances, but she'd been through this with her brother and her dad. All the reassurances in the world hadn't saved them. And she'd never had the chance to hope for a good outcome for Christopher.

She took a deep breath as she followed Hudson into a room in the emergency wing. A pretty redhead with a stricken look on her face bounced a little girl on her lap. A riot of red curls surrounded the child's chubby face. A little boy with big brown eyes and medium brown hair clung to her arm.

"Tiff, I want you to meet my friend Melody Hammond. She's going to take the kids over to the sitter's house."

A tear trickled down Tiffany's cheek. She sniffled. "Thank you. Sharon, the lady who watches them when I'm at work, is expecting you."

Melody wanted to reach out to Tiffany but felt inadequate. Every day she dealt with tragic situations in the lives of the women she helped, but these kinds of events nearly froze Melody's mind. They only created a flood of bad memories, but thinking about herself didn't help anyone.

"Would you like me to pray for Carter?" Melody asked, hoping it was the right thing to say.

Tiffany nodded, and Melody prayed for Carter and the doctors. She silently begged God to spare the life of this young father whose wife and children needed him. Would God answer in the affirmative? She had to believe He would. After she finished praying, she hunkered down beside the chair. "Who do you have here?"

Tiffany sniffled, but smiled. "This is Aubrey, and over here is Carter, Jr., but we call him CJ."

"Will she come to me?" Melody reached out.

Nodding, Tiffany held the little girl out to Melody. She took the child in her arms and stood. Melody breathed a sigh of relief when the little girl didn't make a fuss. "Hi, Aubrey. Would you like to visit with Ms. Sharon this morning?"

The little girl nodded and smiled shyly at Melody. Her heart melted as the child snuggled close. She hadn't thought about having children since Christopher had died. She swallowed hard as a powerful longing inundated her. She shoved the thought from her mind. This wasn't the time to be thinking about herself.

Hudson scooped CJ up in his arms. "You ready to go with Uncle Hudson?"

CJ giggled as Hudson bounced the boy in his arms.

Melody looked over at Hudson. "You're going with me?"

Hudson nodded. "At least to the car. You can't manage two kids and this mammoth diaper bag all by yourself, can you?"

Melody wasn't going to argue with him. "I suppose not."

Hudson grabbed the bag, then turned to Tiffany. "Be back in a few minutes."

Melody followed him as he trotted to the car. He helped her put the kids into their car seats and placed the diaper bag in the front. He handed her the keys and the directions to the babysitter's house as she got into the car.

The whole scene screamed of family.

Hudson. Her. Kids.

She pushed that thought away. There were so many reasons she couldn't go there. Pretty soon her mind would be a blank if she kept banishing her thoughts.

Hudson stood for a moment by the open door. "I'll call you if I learn something new before you get back. Thanks for your help."

Nodding, she started the car and Hudson closed the door. He stood there and watched as she drove away. His caring heart for the man who worked for him brought a lump to Melody's throat. It would be so easy to care about him.

A few minutes later Melody delivered the children to their caregiver. With the kids safely in Sharon's care, she made her way back to the hospital. *Please, Lord, spare Carter's life.* She repeated the prayer over and over as she drove.

While Melody walked through the parking lot to the emergency room, she could see Hudson on the phone and Tiffany in a nearby chair. As Melody stepped through the door, Hudson ended his call and came her way. "Carter's still in surgery."

Melody looked Tiffany's way. Worry still clouded the other woman's features. "How's she holding up?"

"As good as can be expected. She's talked to her parents and Carter's parents. They're on their way to the hospital from Dalton, where they all live. No matter what happens, I plan to stay until they get here." Hudson looked as though he wanted to say something else, but he remained silent as he stared at her.

"That's good. I'm sure she'll appreciate your support." Melody looked toward the parking lot. "I have to get back because I have a meeting with some of my ladies in a half hour."

"Sure. I can't expect you to stay. Thanks for coming and helping out." A muscle worked in his jaw. "I'll call with any news."

"Thanks. I'll be praying." Melody said her goodbyes to Tiffany, giving her a hug.

On the drive back to The Village, Melody continued to pray. The situation had stirred up a lot of emotions for her. She couldn't shake the hurt in her heart. She prayed that Tiffany wouldn't have to deal with the loss of her husband. These circumstances made Melody more determined to keep Hudson at a distance, even though his goodness invited her to let him into her life.

Chapter Seven

Carter had come through the surgery and would eventually recover, but it would be a long process. Hudson didn't know what he would do without the man who knew the ins and outs of the projects they had going, especially the one at The Village. Carter would be absent from work for months. Those months would test Hudson in more ways than he'd ever expected.

Searching for a replacement would take time he didn't have right now. Responsibility for Conrick Construction and its survival lay solely in his hands. A lot of people were counting on him, and he had to come through for all of them.

The image of Melody's face floated across his mind. Her willingness to help out today made him wish he hadn't given her the promise not to ask her out again. He had to be patient and do his best to show her he was a man she could count on—a man she wanted to get to know and spend time with. And so he could get to know her, too, and find out if his impression that she was different from the other women he'd dated was right. He wondered if Melody could be the one woman who could erase the bad memories and hurt that Nicole had left behind.

Would Carter's accident help Melody see that life was uncertain and that playing it safe didn't always result in security?

With these thoughts swirling through his mind, Hudson parked his car near the administration building. He had to keep his mind on the business at hand—the road rally. Melody had offered to talk to him about his plans during her lunchtime. Grateful that she'd agreed to let him bring her lunch, he grabbed the bag containing sandwiches from his favorite deli. Despite the burdens that weighed him down, he had no doubt seeing Melody would lighten his heart.

As Hudson made his way through the reception area, Lovie greeted him. "I'm so sorry to hear about your friend Carter. I'll be praying for him."

"I appreciate that."

Lovie gave him a speculative look. "Are you here to see Ms. Melody?"

"Yes, we have a fund-raising idea to discuss."

Lovie wagged a finger at him. "You should be discussing more than fund-raising. You got to get busy on the romance front. Valentine's Day is right around the corner."

Hudson couldn't help laughing as he shook his head. "Lovie, what am I going to do with you?"

"Follow my advice and romance that woman."

Hudson wanted to tell Lovie that it was easier said than done in Melody's case, but he wasn't about to admit to this grandmotherly matchmaker that he was a flop in the romance department. "Some things can't be rushed."

"I don't know what it is with you young people these

days. When I was a girl, we didn't waste time thinking about love, we did something about it."

"I'll consider your advice." Hudson chuckled as he started down the hall.

"Don't consider it. Act on it," Lovie called after him.

Hudson knocked on Melody's door and wondered whether Lovie had given Melody the same little talk. No matter what Lovie said, he wasn't about to jump into any relationship without making sure there would be no repeat of his former experience with love. At this point, working with Melody would have to suffice for getting to know her and judging whether she was the kind of woman he believed her to be—someone who cared about people, someone who didn't use people for their own advantage.

Melody opened the door. "Are things still okay with Carter?"

"They are, but he'll be in intensive care for a few days." Hudson set the bag of food on Melody's desk. "They're grateful that he's going to pull through, but they know it won't be easy. Tiff's mom will stay with her for a while. That'll help."

Melody nodded. "You were a big help to them today."

"I did what had to be done. Carter and I have known each other for a long time. I helped him get a job with Conrick Industries after we graduated from college."

"He's blessed to have a friend like you." She opened the bag and peered inside. "What did you bring me?"

Hudson tried to digest the compliment from Melody. "I'm doubly blessed to have a friend like him. I brought you a turkey on wheat with tomato, lettuce and provolone cheese, just like you requested."

Opening the container, Melody sat behind her desk

while Hudson sat on the chair on the other side. "You want to give thanks?"

Hudson nodded and bowed his head. He thanked God for Carter's good prognosis and prayed for his recovery, then gave thanks for the food and asked a blessing on their meeting. When he said amen, he looked up to find Melody blinking back tears. He frowned. "What's wrong?"

"Your prayer touched me. It's been an emotional morning for me." She tried to smile while she wiped at her eyes. "This whole thing with Carter reminded me of losing my fiancé, Christopher, and losing my brother and dad. I'm so glad Carter's going to be okay."

"I don't want you to be sad." He reached across the desk and touched her arm. "I know it must have been hard to lose your fiancé in such a horrific manner. The wars in that area of the world have brought sorrow to the military and civilians alike. I appreciate your sharing with me. Are you sure you're all right?"

"Yes." She tried to smile but wound up pressing her lips together obviously trying to ward off more tears. "It's been hard to talk about Christopher, but things get better every year. Thoughts of him still pop into my mind unexpectedly. Carter's accident was a trigger for those sad memories." She picked up her sandwich and took a bite as if to signal the end of the conversation.

For a few moments they ate in silence while Hudson let her admission roll through his mind. He didn't want to press her for details. This was the first time she'd ever mentioned Christopher in his presence. Was it a good sign that she could talk about the loss of the man she had loved? Melody's reference to this tragedy made Hudson see more clearly her reasons for not wanting to date him.

Maybe he did take chances when he raced cars or jumped from planes, but he wasn't ready to give up those things. Wasn't life itself one big chance? A person never knew what the day would hold.

He wished he could convince Melody that her worries were unfounded. He wasn't going into a war zone when he participated in the activities he enjoyed. Could he insinuate himself into her life until those things didn't matter to her anymore? He didn't want to cause her more hurt, so talking about something else was the wise thing to do.

"How'd your meeting go?" Hudson took a bite of his sandwich as he listened to Melody talk about her work. Her enthusiasm touched him deep inside. Everything about her touched him. While they ate, they also talked about the Valentine banquet and discovered that Ian had them working together in the kitchen. Hudson wondered whether she recognized the matchmaking efforts behind their assignments.

Their food gone, Melody brought up the information about road rallies on her computer. "I've read this, and I agree that it sounds like a good idea. Who will determine the route and the time?"

Hudson pointed first to her and then at himself. "We will."

"Us?" Melody's mouth formed a grim line.

"Yes. Adam gave me the go-ahead to help you plan this."

A flicker of annoyance crossed Melody's face. "I wish Adam had consulted me, too. How do we do this?"

"We plan out the route, then we drive it and generate the clues and instructions. After we've determined that, we drive it again and time ourselves. That'll be the official time that someone has to match or come closest to in order to win. We'll also have prizes for gathering certain items along the route—all donated, of course."

"Are you going to solicit them?"

Hudson nodded. "I will."

"Great. When do you plan to drive the route?"

Hudson took a deep breath. "When we have a day off. Maybe this coming Saturday."

She leaned back in her chair with her arms crossed, but she didn't look happy. "There's no racing involved, correct?"

"Correct. We'll drive the speed limit. Variables will be traffic lights and the time it takes each team to interpret the clues, collect any items listed and perform any requested tasks." Hudson raised his eyebrows as he looked at her. "So is this Saturday good?"

"I guess it'll have to be." She let out a long sigh. "When will we hold the event?"

"Sometime in late March or early April. We should allow enough time to get the word out and have people sign up."

"We need to run the dates by Adam, so he can coordinate the calendar and get it in the newsletter and out to area churches and civic groups."

"That sounds like a good strategy." He wasn't going to make a comment on her less-than-enthusiastic acceptance of the plan. He would be thankful that she had agreed. This was as close to a date as he could get without actually asking her to go out with him. Would this time together do anything to cut through the barrier she'd erected to shut him out and put to rest any of his own doubts?

* * *

Ferraris sat in Melody's driveway. The car and the man. She stared out the window as Hudson came up her front walk. She was going to spend the day with him in the close confines of that car. Could her resolve not to let him into her heart survive this scenario?

As soon as Hudson stepped onto her porch, she opened the door. "I'm ready. Got my map and a notebook."

"Let's get started."

He opened the passenger door for her and, as she slid onto the seat, the feel and the smell of leather reminded her of their date. Sitting in this fancy vehicle with its low-slung bucket seats made her heart race. He said they would travel at the speed limit. She clung to that promise.

Hudson folded his lanky frame into the driver's seat. She buckled her seat belt, almost expecting the car to launch itself from the driveway. When the engine thundered, her heart did, too. She shouldn't be afraid to live a little.

He looked her way as he pulled out of her neighborhood onto the main road. "Since we've got the route highlighted on your map, we need to notice landmarks, parks or places of interest where we can ask the participants to collect an item or take a photo of something to bring back. We also want to give some of the route instructions in clue form."

Melody wrinkled her brow. "Are you good at that kind of thing?"

He laughed. "You have to ask?"

She held up her hands in surrender. "The job's yours."

"Of course, I need your final approval."

"Of course." She couldn't hold back her laughter. "I

doubt there are too many times when you have to ask for that."

"Then, you've never met my dad." Hudson shook his head. "I call him the lovable tyrant. I do love him even though he insists on having his way."

Melody wondered about their relationship. Judging from these comments, it sounded somewhat troubled. "Thankfully, we don't need to get his okay."

Hudson let out a belly laugh. "I think he'd like you."

Melody wasn't sure what to make of that statement as a follow-up to his previous one. "I hope so, if I ever meet him."

"There's no doubt you would charm him."

"Thank you. I guess."

"I mean it." Hudson gave her a quick look before focusing on the road. "Let's concentrate on the task at hand. I've contacted some local businesses on the route, and they're willing to provide clues."

"Wonderful!"

Hudson turned onto a less-traveled road running through a wooded area. "I talked with Jordan Montgomery earlier this week. He said we could use their church parking lot for our starting and ending point. We should limit the entries to one hundred cars. What do you think?"

Melody took a deep breath. "Okay."

"Jordan said the church is willing to provide a meal at the end of the rally."

She looked over at him with a smile. "You've been busy. When did you have time to do this and your other work, too?"

He shrugged. "What can I say? I'm amazing."

Melody was beginning to think he was. How long

could she continue to hold him at arm's length? The question bombarded her mind more and more frequently. "Since you're so amazing, have you come up with some fabulous prizes?"

"Of course. When you're as amazing as I am, what can you expect?"

"Okay, amazing man, tell me what you've got." Melody knew he was joking, but every time he said it she found herself thinking that very thing.

She couldn't deny that he was a remarkable man. The work on the women's shelter was humming right along despite Carter's absence. Hudson charmed the older ladies at the senior center whenever he ate lunch there. Even though the thought of it curdled her stomach, she had to smile when he told them he'd take them on a tandem jump when the weather got warmer. Melody could almost see some of them taking him up on the offer.

"I don't remember everything. Lots of gift certificates. The big one is a free tandem jump from the place where I work as a part-time instructor."

"You mean as in skydiving?" Melody couldn't keep the frown out of her voice. "Not everyone thinks that's a fabulous prize."

"I know, so I got some for the less adventuresome folks. How about a day at a spa?"

"Now, that sounds like something I'd like to win."

"I figured as much." He flashed a grin. "Don't worry. There are prizes to suit every age and every taste."

"How will you determine who gets what prize?"

"We'll have a big board at the end of the rally, and the winners of different categories will get to choose what they want. So it's not as if the big winner will be stuck with something they don't like or can't use."

"I'll need a list of the prizes to put in the advertising."

"I'll have it to you Monday."

"Good." Melody tried to relax. Did she dare? She feared letting down her guard in any way would lead to liking this man too much. She couldn't take a chance on a guy who liked to take chances. But she wouldn't think about that today. Her thoughts would center on the road rally and the fund-raising that went with it.

"You got your notebook ready?"

"Writing utensil." She held up her pen, then her notebook. "Paper."

During the morning, they worked out a seventy-mile course that would take the participants through several small towns and the wooded countryside south of Atlanta. Hudson took them down roads that Melody had never traveled, much less heard of. Some of the unusual names lent themselves to excellent clues for folks to decipher. Along the way they talked with several merchants about the rally and got donations. They found landmarks and historic markers to put on the list for photos.

After they finished planning, they stopped for a quick lunch. While they ate they wrote out a set of instructions. Finally, they returned to the church parking lot and drove the route again. This time Melody kept the timer as they went through the instructions, which included having someone take their picture in front of several landmarks. Melody couldn't help thinking they made a good team.

Returning to the parking lot, Hudson pulled to a stop, then turned to her. "So what's our time?"

"Three hours and forty-one minutes." The quantity of time she'd spent with this thrill-seeking man gave her pause because it had been one of the most enjoyable days she'd had lately. In fact, if she looked back over the weeks since she'd first gone out with Hudson, she had to admit that he'd brightened her life. She shoved that thought away as she looked at him. "Is that the official time?"

He nodded. "Record it somewhere, so we can make it official."

"Okay." Melody logged the time into her notes. "I'll give Adam a full report, so he'll have the certified time to announce after everyone has completed the course."

"Good. We're set." He smiled. "Thanks for your help. Today's been a productive day, and I enjoyed your company."

And I enjoyed yours. The words sat on the tip of her tongue, but she wouldn't say them. She wouldn't give him the idea that they could have some kind of relationship. Her conflicting emotions about Hudson were tying her in knots. "I should be thanking you. After all, you're helping The Village in so many ways."

"No thanks needed. Promoting the work you do has been good for me and made me realize I've been thinking too much about myself."

"It's a common malady. I often have the same problem."

"You? I'd never have guessed."

Melody knew her thoughts about Hudson were self-centered. If she let go of them, would she find too much to like about him, even more than she had today? She wasn't ready to admit she was wrong in ignoring her growing attraction to this man. "Thanks again for the help. I guess we should call it a day."

Hudson put his car in gear and drove out of the parking lot. "I've got one more place I want to stop for a donation, and I thought we'd catch a bite to eat there if you don't have plans."

Putting a smile in place, Melody glanced at him. Why was he always making these invitations that bordered on asking her out, but were never actually dates? "I don't have plans, so that sounds good."

"Great. Have you ever eaten at McGurdy's Pizza?"

Melody chuckled. "More times than I can count. It seems to be the choice for everyone at The Village. Dine in and carryout."

"That should bode well for my donation request."

As the sun danced on the treetops, Hudson pulled his car into the parking lot at McGurdy's. The place was crowded on a Saturday evening, but he managed to snag a spot at the back of the lot. Lively conversation and the smell of spices, garlic and baking bread greeted them as they entered. Melody thought they'd have to wait for a table, but the hostess appeared and led them to a booth that the busboy was clearing.

She slid into the booth and wondered what she should talk about while they ate. Surely he didn't want to discuss the fund-raiser after they'd spent the whole day doing that. She certainly didn't want to discuss his skydiving or car racing. "Should we order the same pizza I ordered when you twisted your ankle?"

"That came from here?"

"You didn't recognize it?"

"I was a little out of it that night."

Hudson chuckled. "Maybe just a little."

"Did I thank you for being so kind?"

"You did. You don't remember?"

Melody shrugged. "You know, I was so sleepy. I kept drifting in and out of dreams. I wasn't sure what was reality."

"So you were dreaming about me?"

Melody hoped the dim light in the restaurant would camouflage the heated blush that crept up her cheeks. Why had she even mentioned that night? She couldn't lie. How could she get around his question? He didn't have a clue that she'd been dreaming about kissing him, so why was she getting all worked up about it? "Yeah, I guess I was."

"A good one, I hope."

"Definitely. You were my hero that day."

He gave her a thoughtful smile. "Thanks for saying that. I appreciate it."

"You're welcome." Melody hoped the whole conversation could end on that positive note.

Her wish came true as the waitress appeared.

After they ordered, Hudson leaned back in the booth as he looked at her. "The work on the women's shelter is moving right along. I have a couple of guys who stepped in to take over Carter's role. He's doing well, too, and that's good news."

"It is." Melody realized she'd been so wrapped up with her work and worries that she hadn't followed up with Carter and his family. That would have to change.

"While we're waiting on the pizza, I'm going to talk to the manager about that donation for a road-rally prize." Hudson stepped out of the booth and strode down the aisle.

Melody wondered what the rest of the evening would bring. Did she dare find out more about Hudson beyond his childhood dance lessons and the less-than-perfect relationship with his father?

"We've got another donation," Hudson announced, sliding back into the booth.

"Wonderful. I know lots of people who love the food

here, so that'll be a good prize." Now, what was a safe topic of conversation? If she asked about his time in the Middle East, it would dredge up memories of Christopher. She didn't want to start crying like the day of Carter's accident.

"I forgot to tell you that I asked my dad about the window in the chapel. He confirmed that Maisy Conrick was my great-grandfather's sister, who died when she was only twenty from diphtheria."

"That's so sad. Do you know a lot about your family history?"

Hudson laughed halfheartedly. "I know too much—most of it related to Conrick Industries. My dad never fails to inform me that a Conrick son has always taken over the family business."

Melody gazed at Hudson as a muscle worked in his jaw. "Are you saying your father wants you to run Conrick Industries and you don't want to do it?"

Hudson's mouth curved in a lopsided smile. "That about sums it up."

Did she dare ask him why he didn't want to take over from his father? Was it any of her business? Maybe Hudson saw running the company as a lot of work that he didn't want to tackle, but that thought didn't square with the man she'd come to know. He'd had no trouble working double duty since Carter's accident. Besides the work on the women's shelter, he also had volunteered to take on this road rally. He didn't try to get out of work. He undertook more. "May I ask why you don't want to run the family business?"

That muscle worked in Hudson's jaw as he stared at her. Before he could answer, the pizza arrived. He gave thanks, then helped himself to a slice. The unanswered question hung there like an overripe piece of fruit on a low-hanging branch—so tempting to pick but not necessarily the right thing to do.

They ate in silence for several moments, each seemingly lost in their own thoughts. Melody hoped her question hadn't ruined the evening.

Hudson put his half-eaten slice on his plate and took a big gulp of his drink. Setting the glass down, he looked at her. "Do you actually want to know why I don't want to take over the company?"

"I wouldn't have asked if I didn't."

Hudson let out a heavy sigh. "Here's the deal. When I was in the army, I didn't know whether I'd live to see another day. I realized I'd never figured out who I am or what I wanted. I'd always done what someone told me to do. Take this class. Go to this school or this church. I'd look in the mirror and wonder who the guy was staring back at me. What did he want? Did he know how to make a decision on his own, or did he always have someone telling him what to do? I didn't want to live that way anymore, but when I got out of the army, my dad immediately shipped me off to work for the company overseas. He didn't ask me whether I wanted to do it. He just told me. I promised myself when I got back that I would finally take charge of my life and quit letting my father rule me."

Melody couldn't miss the determination in his eyes or the disapproval in his voice. She couldn't imagine not being able to make her own choices. "Have you told him this?"

"I've let him know I don't want to run the company. My sister Elizabeth wants the job, and I don't understand why he won't give it to her."

"Have you ever thought about taking the job and then handing it over to her?"

A slow smile brightened his features as he shrugged. "I've been so consumed with not wanting it that I never thought of that. It's something I'll consider discussing with my sister."

"I'm glad I could help."

"And I could kiss you, but I won't because that might be treading on territory I promised I wouldn't enter."

The thought of kissing Hudson sent little prickles up her spine. "And you wouldn't want to do that."

"I didn't say I wouldn't want to do it, but I make a habit of keeping my promises."

"That's something I'll remember." The promise she'd made to herself lingered at the back of her mind, but Hudson was slowly shredding it with his kindness and humor as he shared snippets of his life.

He raised his eyebrows and gave her a mischievous grin as if he knew her thoughts. "You know if you ever want to change the way things stand, you only have to tell me."

"I'll remember that, too." How could she forget? Did he sense with every passing day that he was tearing down her resistance?

"Good." He finished eating his pizza and didn't mention his promise again.

On the drive home, Hudson mentioned his plans to visit Carter after church. Melody wondered whether asking to go with him would constitute changing the way things stood between them. She wasn't ready to do that. Arriving at her house, Melody unlocked her door. "I'll see you tomorrow at church."

Hudson nodded. "Sweet dreams."

"Good night." Melody wondered whether he was referring to her admission that she'd dreamed about him. Trying to shake that question away, she watched him walk to his car, his stride confident. She'd failed to keep the promise she'd made to herself not to let this man into her heart. He'd found a place there. Now what was she going to do about it?

Chapter Eight

Red-and-white balloons and streamers hung from the ceiling in the senior center in anticipation of the Valentine banquet for the residents. Hudson placed the last of the pink baskets filled with red roses on one of the tables covered with white tablecloths, then joined a group of high school kids and other volunteers who were eating a quick bite before the banquet began.

He smiled when Melody sat next to him at a table in the kitchen. Despite her somewhat reluctant acceptance of his presence, he was making headway with her. The fact that she was sitting next to him without his urging her said a lot about her possible shift in attitude. He hoped tonight would bring a big change in her perception of him. He couldn't help smiling when she was around.

"You look very nice in your apron." Melody tried to hide a smile.

"Of course I do." He chuckled as he pointed to the front displaying numerous hearts and a printed message that said Kiss the Cook. "Are you going to follow the instructions?"

She made a face and shook her head. "The chef's wife might object."

Hudson laughed. "You don't believe I'm the cook."

"Hardly."

"Even though you won't kiss me, I'll still tell you what a perfect Valentine you make in your red sweater. You look good in red."

Melody looked down at her sweater, then back up at him as if she wasn't quite sure what to say, but a little smile lingered at the corners of her mouth. "Thank you, but flattery still won't get you a kiss."

"I tried, but it wasn't flattery. I meant it." Smiling, Hudson shrugged as he relished the little bit of flirting. She was definitely warming up to him.

As the seniors gathered in the dining hall, he took in the joy permeating through every corner of the room, not only with the residents who were gathered for the banquet but with those who were there to serve them. He looked over at Melody as she motioned for the volunteers to gather around her.

"Okay, everyone, do you know your assignments?" she said as she surveyed the group.

As the workers nodded, he couldn't help thinking that his task was to make this woman happy. He was growing fonder of her with every passing day. He wondered how he could ever have thought she might be like Nicole. Their "nondate" to plan the road rally had proved better than any real date he'd had in years. She deserved happiness, and somehow he wanted to fit into that picture. He hoped tonight's surprise would be only the beginning.

Melody showed the young waiters how to place the plates on the table. Hudson had a suspicion that at least a few of the high school boys had a crush on her. He couldn't blame them.

He spied Ian motioning to him from the kitchen doorway. Hudson tried to be nonchalant as he joined his friend. "Is everything ready?"

Ian nodded. "We're set. You've got a perfect night with above-average temperatures for your surprise."

Hudson stood with his back to where Melody was still giving instructions. "So the plan is to invite everyone outside after the meal's over?"

"Yes, and I still can't believe the Hudson Conrick I used to know has turned into such a romantic."

"Not necessarily a romantic. I just want to make her smile."

"You will." Ian clapped Hudson on the back. "Now we should get this dinner started."

"Yeah. I'm all for that." He turned back toward the preparation area as Ian went into the dining hall.

After Ian said a prayer, the servers brought salads to all the tables. Hudson worked alongside Melody, Kirsten, Brady and some of the other day-shift workers from the nursing home. They made quick work of getting the chicken Parmesan, angel-hair pasta and garlic bread on the plates. While the diners enjoyed the main course, Melody and her crew put the red-velvet cake on plates and set them out for the servers. During dessert, the praise band from the Chapel Church sang and played some romantic songs. Melody mouthed the words to "Close to You" originally sung by The Carpenters, a song he'd heard his mother listen to numerous times.

Hudson had to force himself not to stand next to her and put an arm around her shoulders. Despite all these romantic feelings about her, he had to caution himself against the tendency to jump into a romance like he jumped out of planes. He'd done that with Nicole because he'd thought she was perfect, but she'd been just the opposite. Although he knew with certainty that Melody was nothing like his ex, he still wondered whether he was taking a romantic leap he wasn't ready for.

Thankful for the ending of the song, he joined Ian, Brady and Adam as they sang a barbershop quartet rendition of the Beatles song "When I'm Sixty-Four." When they finished, the place exploded with applause. The four men took a bow, then Hudson returned to the kitchen for the cleanup.

Melody smiled at him. "I didn't know you could sing. You should do that more often."

Hudson shrugged. "It was kind of a last-minute thing that Adam decided we should do."

"It was very good."

"Thanks." He could hardly wait to see her face when she witnessed his surprise.

After the entertainment ended, Ian came to the microphone. "Ladies and gentlemen, we have a special event for everyone tonight if you'd like to join us on the quad. The evening is warm for February, but some of you may still want to grab a jacket before you venture out. Our barbershop quartet will sing another song while everyone gathers near the fountain."

A buzz of conversation filled the hall as folks got up from their chairs or moved their wheelchairs toward the door. Melody looked over at Hudson. "Do you know what this is about?"

"I do."

"Tell me what's going on."

"I can't. It's a surprise." He grinned, his heart pound-

ing with excitement. "You'll find out along with everyone else. Do you need a jacket?"

"I've got one right here." She snagged one from the
back of a nearby chair. "I'm eager to see what's happening."

"Join the crowd." He gestured for her to go ahead
while he stepped behind her.

Stars sparkled in the darkened sky, and a sliver of a
moon graced the treetops. He took a deep breath as he
tried to calm himself. He didn't think he'd be this nervous. Surely, she would love this.

"It's a beautiful night."

"It is." He motioned toward the fountain, sporting sil-
ver balloons and flowing with red water. "I've got to join
the quartet."

"Go ahead."

For the next few minutes the quartet performed "Some-
body to Love." After the song ended, applause echoed
across the quad, and Hudson took in Melody's smile with
a happy heart. Did he dare trust that God had brought her
into his life for a reason? His attendance at the Chapel
Church had brought him closer to God and renewed his
faith that had been dormant for the past few years. Working at The Village had showed him what putting faith into
action was all about.

Was it time to rethink his wishes to keep skydiving
and racing cars? If he quit doing those things, would that
endear him to Melody? He wasn't sure that was the answer. Making those changes might put him right back
where he didn't want to be—having someone else dictate
his choices in life. But he didn't need to make any decisions tonight. He only wanted to enjoy watching Melody
in the next few minutes.

As the applause died and the crowd quieted, Ian stepped to the front of the group. "Thanks, everyone. Let's give a big round of applause for our servers and volunteers who have made this evening fantastic."

Again applause filled the air. Then Ian waved to quiet the gathering. "We are truly blessed to have a lot of wonderful people who live and work here in The Village. Tonight I want to thank one special person." Ian motioned for Hudson to step forward. "Hudson Conrick and his company have been renovating one of our buildings so we can expand our women's ministries. He has something he'd like to share with you this evening."

Hudson turned to face the crowd. He surveyed the joy radiating from the faces illuminated by the lights from the fountain and the quad. "Thanks, Ian. It's been my pleasure to work here and get to know many of you. Not long after I started the work here, I learned that there's a bell in the chapel steeple. It's been silent for a long time because the mechanism for ringing it has been broken. Tonight we're going to change that."

A murmur went through the group, and Hudson looked over at Melody. With her fingertips on her mouth, she gazed up at the steeple. Then she glanced at him, an expression of awe brightening her features. She dropped her hand as she smiled.

Giving Ian the signal, Hudson also turned his gaze. In the next second spotlights flooded the spire and the bell began to ring, its booming tones reverberating across the campus. A spontaneous cheer rippled through the gathering, followed by applause that accompanied the chiming bell. Hudson glanced Melody's way. She was walking toward him.

Tears glistened in her eyes as she stopped in front of him. "You're responsible for this?"

He nodded, his heart thundering along with the ringing bell. "As soon as you told me about it, I knew I had to fix it for you."

Standing on her tiptoes, she threw her arms around his neck and hugged him. He gently held her in his arms and wished he never had to let her go. He wanted to lift her off the ground and twirl her around in a circle, but he resisted the urge.

She stepped away, her hand over her heart. "That's the nicest thing anyone has ever done for me. Thank you. Thank you. I can never thank you enough."

He wished he could tell her that she could thank him by not keeping him on the edges of her life. But he feared ruining this good moment between them.

The sound of the bell brought out residents from the women's shelter, the children's homes and even the nursing home. The quad became a sea of celebration. Folks lingered near the fountain even after the bell stopped ringing. Hudson took in the joy with a renewed appreciation for all he had in life. Sharing it had filled a lot of hearts with happiness, especially Melody's. That was worth everything.

Luxury cars of every description lined the circular drive as Melody pulled her aging gray sedan to a stop in front of the Conrick mansion. Hudson had told her that he'd spent very little time in this house because his parents had moved here after he'd started attending a military prep school when he was fourteen. She couldn't imagine leaving home at such an early age. Hudson had never said whether he'd liked the situation, but it was probably part of doing as he was told.

Three weeks had passed since the Valentine banquet and Hudson's surprise gift. Her heart still melted at his thoughtfulness. With what seemed like a rather formal and cold upbringing, how had he become the warm-hearted man she'd come to know? Maybe she would find out today.

With her stomach tied in knots, she approached the mammoth house with its massive front door. The leaded glass sparkled in the sunlight. What would she find on the other side? Would a butler answer when she rang the bell?

Holding her breath, Melody prayed that all would go well. Yet despite her prayer, the old feelings of inadequacy engulfed her as she stood there waiting for someone to answer the door. Would these women look down at her with pity? Would they talk about her behind her back after she left? Why did she still let her experiences from high school color her perceptions? She was a grown woman, a child of God, and He valued every person—rich or poor. It didn't matter what these people thought.

She tried to let that idea permeate her mind, but she couldn't forget that, in a sense, it did matter what they thought of her. She wanted to represent The Village in a positive light. Today she was the face of The Village. She had to make the best of this invitation from Hudson's mother to tell her ladies' group about these ministries.

A shadowy figure approached the door. When it opened, a woman of medium height with carefully coiffed brunette hair smiled and extended her hand. "Welcome, Melody. I'm Susan Conrick. We're so glad you could share with us today."

Melody's nervousness melted under the warm greeting

as a heartfelt smile curved her mouth. God was answering her prayer already. "Thanks for having me."

"Come join the rest of the ladies in the solarium." Susan gestured toward the back of the house. "I've been eager to meet you. Hudson has said so many wonderful things about you and The Village."

"We're grateful for the work he's doing to expand our women's shelter. It's going well." Melody wasn't sure what to think about Hudson talking about her with his mother.

He'd become part of her daily life, but he'd kept his promise not to ask her for another date. She was the one who had insisted it be that way. So why did it bother her that he was abiding by her wishes? But this meeting with his mother wasn't the time to examine that question.

"We thought it would be nice to enjoy the solarium room on a sunny day even though the temperatures outside are chilly. Our weather this winter has been quite crazy—warmer than normal one week and frigid the next."

"Yes, it has. March definitely came in like a lion." Melody took a calming breath. The weather was always an easy topic of conversation.

Susan chuckled as she led the way through the well-accessorized living room and past the huge kitchen accented with granite countertops and with built-ins of every kind. "Let's hope it goes out like a lamb."

"That's my thinking, too." Melody tried not to gawk at the display of wealth surrounding her. She prayed not to be judgmental or envious. The two seemed to go hand in hand. "Your home is beautiful."

"Thank you. We enjoy it."

Who wouldn't? Melody pushed the thought away.

Lord, I need Your help in all kinds of ways today. Keep my mind focused on You.

As they drew near to the solarium, the sound of laughter and conversation drifted their way. Susan stopped and turned to Melody. "Everyone's eager to hear what you have to say, but first we're going to enjoy lunch."

"That's fine. I'll give my talk whenever you're ready." She tried to produce a genuine smile, but she couldn't vanquish the fake one that curved her lips. The nerves had returned.

Susan didn't move but turned and looked Melody right in the eye. "I hope you don't feel as though I'm trying to put you on the spot. I understand if you feel a bit nervous, but there's no need. This is a lovely group of women, and we want to know how we can help your ministry. Treat us like old friends."

Melody didn't know quite how to respond. The woman had obviously recognized the nervous smile. "Thanks for trying to put me at ease."

Susan nodded and forged ahead around the corner.

Melody nearly stopped in her tracks when the solarium came into view. Sunshine beamed through the glass ceiling and windows of the enclosure and reflected off the white marble floors, making the place look like a crystal palace. An oval glass-topped table, large enough to accommodate over a dozen people, sat at the far end of the room. Fine china and crystal goblets adorned the table. Spider plants hung from the beams in the ceiling while foliage of every description filled each corner. This marvelous room looked out on the pool that sparkled in the sunlight. Melody had never seen such a beautiful room.

The chatter stopped when Susan stepped across the threshold and walked through the seating area filled with rattan couches and chairs with colorful overstuffed cushions and glass-topped end tables. "Ladies, our guest has arrived. I'd like you to welcome Melody Hammond, women's director at The Village of Hope Ministries."

Melody nodded, smiled and prayed again. She could do this. She'd spoken at hundreds of events like this before. "Thank you for inviting me."

Susan motioned to a chair at one end of the table. "Let's have you sit here."

She nodded as she sat on the padded chair. "Thank you."

"Let's say a prayer of thanksgiving for our food, and then we'll make some introductions." Susan sat in the empty chair to Melody's right.

After the prayer, each lady introduced herself, and Melody employed her memory techniques to remember at least each first name. During the introductions, two women dressed in uniforms quietly rolled a cart into the room and began serving the salads—a combination of greens and fruit.

As they worked their way through the different courses, the women traded stories about their latest trips abroad and their grandchildren. Melody smiled and nodded and laughed at the appropriate times, but she had little to contribute to the conversation. It only served as a reminder to her that she didn't fit into this world. She'd hoped not to feel this way, but it happened every time she had to attend such an event.

After everyone had finished eating, Susan stood. "I hope y'all enjoyed the lunch. We'll go to the seating area for Melody's presentation."

A murmur of agreement accompanied the group as they made their way across the room. Melody congratulated herself when she remembered each lady's name. After everyone was seated, she passed out brochures outlining the ministries at The Village. The women took a few moments to look over the information, then listened while she explained the services.

She finished her talk and asked for questions. Soon a lively conversation ensued and Melody's nerves vanished as she talked about the things that were dearest to her heart and how God worked wonders in so many lives at The Village. As she answered questions, she realized she'd been all wrong about not fitting into their world. She might not have the same lifestyle, but they shared one thing—the desire to help others.

By the time she had finished, she had more volunteers for The Village shop and more monetary pledges for the expansion of the women's shelter. Today's meeting had turned out better than she'd ever expected. She should have known God would make everything good.

Susan came up to Melody as the others were leaving. "Please stay for a moment, so we can talk some more. If you have time."

"I do." Melody wondered what else Hudson's mom had to say. Susan ushered Melody back into the solarium. "We might as well make ourselves comfortable here."

Melody sat on one of the colorful couches and tried to relax. "What did you want to talk about?"

"First, I wanted to tell you how much I enjoyed your presentation. You did a wonderful job."

"Thanks. It's always a blessing to share the work of The Village."

"I can tell it's something you really care about." Susan hesitated for a moment. "I'd like for you to share the same things with my whole family next weekend. It's my husband's birthday, and we always have a big celebration. Would you be able to join us on Saturday for dinner?"

Melody wondered why Susan couldn't tell her family about The Village herself, or why her son couldn't do it. Was she trying to promote a relationship between her and Hudson? Surely not. Melody doubted that she fit the profile of the ideal woman for Hudson—one who shared his social circle. She shouldn't second-guess the reasons for this request. She should be glad for the opportunity. "I think I'm free, but I need to double-check my calendar and get back to you."

"Excellent." Susan settled back on the couch. "Tell me a little about yourself."

Melody tried not to read anything into the conversation, but she couldn't help wondering whether Susan was trying to get information because she suspected her son had an interest in a woman who didn't fit into their world. "There isn't much to tell."

Susan waved a hand at Melody. "I'm sorry. That was really too open-ended. Did you grow up in Atlanta?"

Melody shook her head. "I'm from a small town in southern Georgia. My mother still lives there."

"Do you get back to visit her very often?"

"Probably not as often as I should. I've tried to get her to move to this area, but she doesn't like big cities."

"She sounds like my mother. Bless her soul. We lived on a farm in South Georgia, and she never understood why I would want to live here. But I went to college and fell in love with a city boy."

"How do you feel now about living in an urban area?"

"I don't mind, but you must admit that our house isn't exactly in the city." Smiling, Susan shrugged. "It's kind of the best of both worlds."

"You do have a good bit of privacy here."

"When my parents passed away, they gave Hudson the farm because he was the only grandson. You see, I was an only child. My parents wanted more children, but it wasn't meant to be, so they were thrilled when I gave them four grandchildren. They doted on Hudson. The girls got money, and Hudson got the land."

Hudson owned a farm. Melody wondered whether it was close to her hometown. What did it matter? She had no interest in the man. At least that's what she kept telling herself. "What does he do with it?"

"The farm is made up of a lot of timberland, and he pays a manager to take care of it. We sometimes go down there for long weekends. The big, old rambling house where I lived as a child is still on the property. That's where we stay. Sometimes Hudson rents out the house during hunting season."

Melody chatted with Susan for several more minutes about nothing of much importance. Finally, she excused herself, but as Melody stepped onto the front porch, Susan acted as though she wanted to say something else. In the end she must have thought better of it.

Walking to her car, Melody wished she knew what was on the older woman's mind. Did it have anything to do with Hudson, or was it something of little consequence?

Hudson's mother was warm and charming. He must have taken after her rather than his father. Melody kept telling herself that she didn't want to become involved with a man who participated in dangerous activities, but she was finding it harder and harder to convince herself that Hudson's interest in those things was so terrible. But fear continued to niggle at the back of her mind whenever she thought of throwing caution aside and embracing a relationship with the handsome risk taker.

Chapter Nine

"We're here. I hope you enjoy the evening," Hudson said after parking his car in front of his parents' house.

"You sound doubtful."

"Didn't mean for it to come across that way." He gave Melody a lopsided grin, hoping he wouldn't have to take back his statement. His mom would make the evening wonderful even though he suspected she was matchmaking. That didn't bother him, but what his dad might do concerned Hudson. The man could be charming but foreboding and unpredictable, as well.

Hudson walked Melody to the front door and prayed for a positive outcome for this party. For many years he'd dreaded attending his father's birthday party. Too many times H.P. had used his birthday party to give Hudson new marching orders. Would that happen tonight, despite their recent talk?

For many of the recent ones, he'd been overseas and unable to attend. He couldn't get out of this one, and to make things worse, his mother had invited Melody so she could tell the whole family about The Village.

He didn't mind that she was coming with him or that

she'd asked him to share his project, but he feared what kind of pronouncement his father would make on the occasion of his sixty-eighth birthday. Hudson didn't want to argue with his father in front of company. In front of family was bad enough. Hudson could only hope the event would be one of celebration, peace and harmony. Even though he had numerous disagreements with his father, Hudson loved the man. He wanted Melody to like his family, too.

The door opened before they reached the front porch. His mother stepped out and gave him a hug, then turned to Melody. "Welcome. I'm so glad you could join us."

"Me, too."

Hudson watched for that tight smile that so often formed on Melody's lips when she was trying to make you believe she was happy. But tonight her smile was genuine, and that buoyed his spirits. Maybe tonight wouldn't be so bad after all. "So where's the birthday boy?"

Susan looped her arm through her son's. "He's waiting for you in the sitting room. Your sisters and the rest of the family have already arrived."

"Then, we can make our grand entrance." Hudson laughed halfheartedly.

Susan glanced over at Melody. "Don't listen to him. There will be no grand entrances. As soon as he walks into that room, he'll be smothered with nieces and nephews."

Shrugging, Hudson laughed again. "What can I say? They love me."

"They adore him, but he shouldn't let it go to his head. They like their grandmother more." Susan nodded as she patted his arm. "Hudson, will you put your jackets in the coat closet?"

"Sure." Hudson helped Melody out of her jacket. "We've had such a mild winter, but I hear a cold front's headed our way tomorrow."

"I'm afraid so." Susan grimaced.

As they made their way toward the sitting room, he wondered what Melody was thinking. She'd already met his mother, but he was afraid the tension with his father would spill over into the rest of the family. But for now, laughter and lively conversation greeted them as they approached the French doors that led to the room. True to his mother's word, the children came running as soon as they spied him.

"It's Uncle Hud." His five-year-old nephew, Riley, raced toward them.

Hudson picked the boy up and tossed him over his shoulder. "I've got you captured now."

The boy squealed and wriggled to get down, and Hudson quickly set him on the floor. In the next instant, the other kids surrounded him as he hunkered down to greet the littlest ones. Then he stood and gave the older kids a fist bump. "Hey, gang, I want you to meet someone."

"Is she your girlfriend?" Riley's older brother Jacob asked.

Hoping the warmth creeping up his neck wasn't a blush, Hudson shook his head. "No, young man, she's my boss, and you'd better be nice to her."

The boy's eyes grew wide as he nodded vigorously. "I will, Uncle Hud."

A collective laugh rippled through the room as he took Melody's elbow and guided her farther into the room. "Melody, let me introduce you to my family."

She smiled at him, but he could read the uncertainty in her eyes. "I hope you won't test me on all the names."

Susan stepped forward. "You did a marvelous job remembering all my friends a few weeks ago. They were impressed."

Melody shrugged as she let out a seemingly self-conscious laugh. "It was nothing."

Hudson leaned closer to her and whispered, "You don't have to remember all these people."

She smiled up at him. "Thanks. I appreciate that, but I'll try."

"You can remember my name." Hudson's youngest niece, a sweet little girl with curly dark hair, planted herself in front of Melody. "My name's Madelyn. Uncle Hud calls me Maddie."

"Is it okay if I call you Maddie, too?" Melody asked.

His niece nodded. "I think it'll be okay since you're his boss."

"Thanks, Maddie," Melody replied as another ripple of laughter spread through the room.

Hudson looked at her. "Now that you've met my youngest sister's kids, are you ready for the full introductions?"

Taking a deep breath, she nodded, that nervous little smile curving her mouth.

He motioned toward the chair where his father sat. "My father, H.P."

His dad stood and took one of Melody's hands in his. "It's nice to meet you. I understand you're the little lady who's in charge of the project my son's involved with."

"Yes, sir." Melody nodded. "Happy birthday."

"Thank you. I'm trying to be happy about being another year older." H.P.'s voice boomed across the room. "Is that son of mine doing good work?"

"The best." Melody took a step back when H.P. released her hand.

Hudson tried not to let Melody's approval go to his head. She was kind enough not to say anything negative to his father. His dad, on the other hand, wasn't so generous with his praise.

Hudson motioned to the rest of his family sitting or standing around the room. "Now for the rest of this gang. My eldest sister, Elizabeth, and her husband, Todd, and their two kids, Alex and Melissa."

"It's nice to meet you." Elizabeth flashed Hudson an irritated smile. "Of course, he had to put in that bit about my being the eldest."

Hudson grinned. "She might as well know who has seniority."

"Seniority with what? I'd like to know," Elizabeth said.

"With everything. You know you've loved bossing me around since I was old enough to understand what you were saying."

"I can't deny that." Elizabeth winked at Melody.

He was thankful that Elizabeth had gone along with his joke. Sometimes she could be like their father—too serious and unbending. Maybe that was why his dad was reluctant to hand the reins over to her. The two of them were too much alike. His two younger sisters took after their mother, who was much more easygoing and quite flexible. He continued the introductions with his middle sister, Julie, and her husband, Sean, and their three children, Hannah, Shelby and Hunter. Moving on, he finished with his youngest sister, Rebecca, and her husband, Justin.

Smiling, Susan stepped to the center of the room.

"Now that we've inundated Melody with names, let's go into the dining room for the delicious dinner Sarah has prepared."

With Melody at his side, Hudson hung back while his family filed out of the room. He wondered what she thought about the people he loved. "Was that a little overwhelming?"

"I think I can remember all the names, but not which child belongs with which parent."

"I won't give you a test."

"That's good." She chuckled as she matched his stride. "You have a nice family."

"Until you really get to know them." Hudson stopped just outside the dining room.

Melody frowned at him. "Is that any way to talk about them?"

"I was only kidding, but I'll admit I don't always see eye to eye with them."

"Do any of us always agree with everything our families do?"

"You know that's the case with me, but I promise I won't mention it again this evening." He offered her his arm. "Let's go eat."

She slipped her arm through his, and like the night of the fund-raiser, he felt like the luckiest man in the room. He was with the most beautiful woman. He escorted her to the table and pulled out her chair, then took the one next to her. They sat at the end by the head of the table where his dad sat occupying his chair like a head of state. Before the meal, H.P. asked Hudson to offer a prayer as everyone joined hands. He glanced over at Melody as he held out his hand. This was one time when he didn't mind bowing to his father's command. When she placed her hand in his, memories of her spontaneous hug from the night of the Valentine banquet poured into his mind. He took a deep breath as he focused his thoughts on prayer, not on the soft, feminine hand holding his.

As soon as Hudson finished, Sarah and her kitchen help brought out the first course, one of H.P.'s favorites, shrimp cocktail.

His dad took the first bite, then laid aside his fork. "Now, this is the way to start a birthday party."

Laughter spread around the table as everyone joined him. Everything from the appetizer to the perfectly grilled steaks pleased his father. As he finished off the last morsel of his steak, H.P. leaned toward Melody. "A man should be allowed to have steak more than once a year on his birthday."

Hudson took in Melody's deer-in-headlights expression and jumped in to rescue her from his dad's complaints. "Dad, you know that's what the doctor ordered."

H.P. frowned. "It's criminal with all the good steak in this world that I can't enjoy it more often. The food police take the enjoyment out of life."

Elizabeth patted her father's arm. "Now, Daddy, calm down. You don't want to raise your blood pressure on your birthday. Think happy thoughts."

H.P. harrumphed and crossed his arms. "My happy thoughts would include more steak."

"How about some birthday cake and ice cream," Sarah said as she wheeled in a cart with a large cake covered with creamy frosting and walnuts. "Carrot cake. Your favorite."

While Sarah served, Hudson wondered what would make his dad happy besides his favorite foods. Did he find joy in telling other people what to do? Was that why he pushed his only son? Was his attitude what led to his success?

What would happen if he slipped out from under his father's thumb? He could do that if he put Elizabeth in charge, but would it be the right thing to do? He'd thought Melody's suggestion was brilliant until he'd had time to think it over. That solution would upset his dad and, despite the desire to be his own man, a nagging thought plagued Hudson. He didn't want to displease the most important man in his life.

Hudson warred with himself over his father's demands. He didn't want to take over the company. If he wanted to be true to himself, he had to stand up to him no matter what the consequences would be. Was that what he wanted?

Susan tapped on her water goblet with a spoon, shaking Hudson from his troubling thoughts. "Let's sing 'Happy Birthday'."

H.P. waved a hand and knit his eyebrows, but Hudson could tell that underneath his father's objection there was a happy man. His mom had always been able to bring out the best in her husband. Without a doubt, his father loved and cherished the woman he'd married over forty years ago. Hudson wondered whether he could find a love like that. He'd made a wrong decision with Nicole. Was Melody a better choice? He wished she'd let him find out.

As they sang, Hudson glanced around the table at the happy faces of his family. When they finished singing, his gaze stopped on Melody, and his pulse pounded as he swallowed a lump in his throat. He'd been telling himself for weeks that he should be cautious where she was concerned. But it hadn't mattered. His heart couldn't resist the onslaught of her beauty, her giving nature and her love for people of all kinds.

But he couldn't break his promise. He had to let her take the lead or convince her to change her mind about that second date.

Melody fought back the emotions that bubbled to the surface as she took in the joy in the room. Hudson's dad reminded her so much of her own—the way he'd grumbled about the food restrictions. She still missed him all these years after he'd died and wished that he could have lived to see his sixty-eighth birthday.

She'd been wrong to tell Hudson to take over the company and then give control to his sister. It would be deceitful unless Hudson told his dad up-front. Melody could see that H.P. doted on his son, whether Hudson could see it himself or not. She also understood why they didn't always get along. They were both strong personalities who had their own way of thinking. Even though Hudson didn't always see his father's point of view, she surmised from their interaction that he respected the older man and wanted to please him. That was probably why it had taken Hudson so long to strike out on his own. She wanted to help.

After everyone had finished dessert, Susan stood and clanged her glass again. "We're going into the solarium and have coffee if you'd like, and while we do that, Melody will tell us about The Village. The younger kids may go to the playroom, but I'd like the older ones to stay and hear what she has to say. I believe there are opportunities for community service there."

"But, Susu, when will Grampy open his presents?" Maddie asked.

"He'll do it after the talk." She patted them each on the head. "I'll call you when he's ready to open his gifts."

Satisfied with their grandmother's answer, the younger children raced off, and Susan smiled. "Such energy. I wish I could bottle it."

H.P. put an arm around his wife. "You have plenty of energy. If you had any more, I couldn't keep up with you."

Susan laughed, and the two walked arm in arm as they led the way to the solarium.

Hudson came up beside Melody as the group followed behind his parents. "So are you having a good time?"

"Yes. The food was amazing. I can understand why your dad complained about not getting to eat it often enough."

H.P. stopped and turned to Melody. "I heard that, young lady. You should talk to my wife and convince her that I shouldn't be on such a restricted diet."

Melody shook her head. "I couldn't do that. I think your wonderful wife loves you and wants to keep you around for a while longer. That's why she makes you watch what you eat."

H.P. nodded. "Yeah. That's what she tells me all the time."

"Listen to her. I lost my granddaddy to a heart attack because he didn't do the things he was told." Melody took in H.P.'s frown and wondered if she'd overstepped. The statement had popped out of her mouth before she'd had the chance to really think it through.

"I am so sorry, my dear." H.P. sighed. "I guess you're right. I should listen to my wife."

She breathed a sigh of relief. Now she could give her talk without that worry.

While everyone jockeyed for a seat, Susan pointed

to a chair with a flaming red cushion. "Melody, please sit here."

"Thanks." Melody wasn't sure what Susan expected from this talk and said a silent prayer for God's guidance.

Hudson immediately grabbed a spot at the end of the sofa next to her chair. When he smiled, her insides scrambled. How could she keep her mind on her talk when he was sitting there smiling at her? She had to focus on his family and not on him, but he kept coming into her line of vision. After everyone was settled, Melody figured she might as well put Hudson front and center since she couldn't get him off her mind. She started her talk with his undertaking at The Village and asked him to give them more details.

Hudson grinned as he looked her way. "She warned me that she planned to put me on the spot, but I'm happy to report that we're halfway finished with the project. Despite Carter's absence, we've been able to maintain our original timeline."

As Hudson continued to talk about his work, Melody believed he was not only sharing with his family, but he was making sure his dad knew what was happening. After Hudson finished, she thanked him and praised his work. She wanted to let him know how much she appreciated what he was doing. She continued her talk by mentioning the different facets of the ministry and put an emphasis on areas where they needed volunteers. Finally, she put in a plug for the road rally.

That topic created a cacophony of conversation throughout the room. Finally, H.P. rapped his knuckles on the nearby table. "We should participate in this fund-raising endeavor."

His pronouncement started another round of conversation. Melody liked the lively interaction between the members of Hudson's family, and she was happy that his dad approved of the idea.

While she watched the commotion, Hudson leaned closer. "You're a hit with my dad. I knew he'd like you."

"The road rally is a hit, and that was your idea."

"True, but I still say he's eager to participate because he likes you."

Eventually, the talk died down and H.P. took over the floor as he gathered commitments for the rally from his children and grandchildren. Melody passed out the forms she'd purposely brought with her. Soon someone from each family group was filling one out.

Hudson leaned an elbow on the arm of the sofa. "I should've known my dad would eventually take over this event."

"That's okay. It's his birthday."

Hudson laughed. "Yes, we must indulge the birthday boy. At least his declaration didn't involve me this year."

Melody wrinkled her brow. "Does it usually?"

Hudson gave her a crooked smile. "Too often."

"And what does he say about you?"

Hudson laughed again. "He tells me what I'm to do next with my life. But that won't happen this year, even if he eventually gets around to such a decree."

Melody wasn't sure how to respond to his statement. Despite the congenial nature of the evening, the conflict between father and son had not subsided. Melody wished she could smooth away the troubles between Hudson and his father, but she would be asking for trouble of her own if she did.

As the leaders of each group finished filling out the

entry forms, they handed them to Melody and expressed their excitement about the event.

H.P. handed her his form, then motioned her toward the door. "Since you're here, come with me to my study. I'll write a check for our entry fee."

"If you'd like to open your gifts in the study, we can bring them in there," Susan said.

"Whatever you'd like, my dear."

Again, Melody tried not to gawk at the affluence surrounding her. These folks took for granted the wealth that was an everyday part of their lives. She immediately shut down her negative thoughts. Hudson's family had shown her today that they were willing to help The Village, not only with their money, but with their time. She should have only good things to think about them. After spending so much time with Hudson, shouldn't she know by now that his wealth wasn't what defined him or his family?

When they reached the double doors that opened into the study, H.P. stood aside to let his wife, daughters and Melody go first. She glanced around the room at the hundreds of books in the built-in bookcase. Dozens of family photos were on display while a massive desk dominated the floor space.

Before Melody finished looking around, H.P. handed her a check. "Here you are."

"Thanks so much. I hope you enjoy the rally." Melody looked up at H.P. "Hudson told me that one of the windows in the Chapel Church at The Village was dedicated to one of your relatives, Maisy Conrick."

"Yes, that's right." He motioned for her to follow as he moseyed over to an old black-and-white photo on one of the walls. "Maisy was my great-aunt. I never knew her because she died before I was born, but family stories are full of her charity and bravery. She went to work among the poor immigrants in New York City. That's where she contracted the diphtheria that killed her. The vaccine for the disease was only in development at the time."

Susan stepped toward them. "The Conrick family history is filled with folks who have been eager to help those who are less fortunate. You should have Hudson tell you about them."

Hudson frowned. "Mom, that would be a little over-the-top. Like, 'Hey, look at us and all the good stuff we do.'"

Susan gave her son an indulgent smile. "I didn't mean it that way."

"We won't talk about it now. It's time for Dad to open his presents." Hudson picked up one of the gaily wrapped gifts.

"I'll agree with that." H.P. sat behind his desk as Hudson handed his dad the gift.

The younger children sprinted into the room and found seats on the floor while the rest of the family sat on the sofa, chairs and window seat. As H.P. ripped the paper from the packages or dug into a gift bag, Melody took in the simple items that brought a smile to his face, especially the handmade gifts from the children. Even those from the adults were simple things that were more sentimental than anything else, such as photos of his grandchildren or of family vacations that were set in special and unusual frames.

All this familial happiness made Melody realize that despite their wealth, the Conricks were like so many throughout the country. They loved each other, but they didn't always agree. The love they shared brought them through the troubled times, even the disagreements.

When H.P. was done, Melody inquired about the location of the restroom and Susan gladly escorted her. After Melody was done there, she wandered back toward the study. As she passed down the hallway, she heard someone say her name. She stopped. Although she knew it wasn't right to eavesdrop, she couldn't help listening.

"What do you know about her?"

"Not much, but Hudson's smitten."

"He's fallen for a gold digger before. Who's to say she isn't another one like Nicole? He's always been a sucker for pretty blondes. And she's very pretty."

"Did you see the way she was buttering up Daddy by taking an interest in the family history? She had him eating out of her hand with that poor-little-me act about her granddaddy. Looks as if she's trying to worm her way into the family."

"Hudson cares about her, and you're too critical. Give her a chance."

"A chance to break Hudson's heart?"

"It's not our business."

"I don't care what you say. I'm making it my business. You can't stop me."

Melody wasn't sure who was talking. The sisters tended to sound alike, especially since she didn't know them that well. One of them seemed to be defending her while the other two were adamant that a poor girl from southern Georgia was surely after Hudson's money. What could she do? The only wise thing right now was to retreat to the bathroom and hope the conversation would be over when she came back out. Or maybe they'd staged the conversation in hopes that she would hear it. Was that their plan?

Back in the beautifully appointed guest bath, Melody stared at herself in the mirror. The old hurts from her high school years stole back into her mind. It was the mean rich girls all over again. They were talking about her behind her back. They didn't believe she was good enough for their brother. Tears welled in Melody's eyes as she continued to look in the mirror. She couldn't go back out there until she got her emotions under control. She wasn't sure how she could push aside the anger, hurt and humiliation. If only they knew that Hudson's money was one of the things that had kept her from falling for him the first time they met. She wouldn't let them win. After wiping her tears, she refreshed her makeup. With her head held high, she made her way back to the study. When she entered the room, Hudson immediately came to her side.

He grinned down at her. "I thought you'd gotten lost."

"I could have in this house. No telling where I might have ended up if I'd taken a wrong turn."

"I would've come looking for you."

"Trying to play my knight in shining armor again?"

"If you want to be my damsel in distress?"

"Not really. No more twisted ankles for me."

"Then, you've got to learn to slow down." He leaned a little closer. "And let me catch you."

Melody's heart tripped. He was flirting with her right here in front of his family. What would his sisters say? "I can't let that happen."

"You could. You should try it, and see how you like it."

Melody was so tempted to do exactly that. She would show his sisters that she was good enough, better than good enough for their brother. Taking a calming breath, she tamped down her anger. That was no reason to pursue Hudson. She didn't want this evening to end on a sour note, but how could it get better when his sisters' hurtful words kept pushing their way back into her thoughts?

"I know the idea of letting me catch you can be overwhelming, but you could say something." Hudson winked at her.

"I'm helping you keep your promise."

Hudson pretended to wipe his brow. "Thanks for saving me."

Melody laughed, thankful for something to blunt the hurt of his sisters' unkind words. "Anytime."

"All right, everyone, we're headed back to the solarium." H.P.'s booming voice gathered their attention. "It's tradition time. One big game of Uno coming up."

"My dad's favorite game. We play it every year on his birthday." Hudson put a hand to Melody's back and guided her toward the door. "I'm making sure you don't get lost."

"I can find my way."

"I'm helping you play it safe."

She gave him an impish smile. "This coming from the man who likes to live dangerously?"

He shrugged. "What can I say? You're influencing my behavior."

If only that was true. Melody smiled but kept the thought to herself.

As the group sauntered back to the solarium, Elizabeth latched on to Hudson's arm. "Hey, little brother. I need a word with you." Elizabeth turned to Melody. "You don't mind if I borrow him for a few minutes?"

Melody pasted on a smile. "He's not mine to lend."

"That's a good one." Elizabeth looked at Melody with a smile nearly as affected as her own, then steered Hudson away.

Melody stood there, not quite sure she was going to find much pleasure in the rest of the evening. But she would. She would not be intimidated. Straightening her shoulders, she entered the solarium, where H.P. and his sons-in-law readied the table for the game.

While Melody watched, Rebecca came over. "So has our family overwhelmed you yet?"

Melody wondered why Rebecca had sought her out. Was she going to tell her to leave Hudson alone? "Not really. I come from a large family myself. I grew up in a small town, and it seemed as though half the town was related to me."

"That sounds like where our mom grew up."

"Yes, she mentioned that when I was here to talk to her ladies' missionary group."

"Mom was very impressed with your presentation."

"Thank you." Melody didn't know what to make of these compliments or Rebecca's seemingly friendly nature.

"I know this isn't any of my business, but I have to say it. Hudson is clearly captivated with you, and I think you should give my little brother a chance."

Melody didn't know what to say, especially after the earlier conversation she'd overheard. Was Rebecca the one who'd been defending her? "I don't understand."

"I shouldn't be telling you this, but a few weeks ago Hudson asked me for advice about women. He didn't mention any names, but now I believe he was asking because of you."

As Melody listened to Rebecca, the hurtful conversation replayed itself in her mind. Nothing made sense. What would Rebecca say if she knew Melody had heard them talking. One way to find out. "Are you sure your sisters would be happy if they knew you were saying this to me?"

"What do my sisters have to do with this?"

"I wasn't meaning to listen, but I—"

"You heard us talking?"

Melody nodded.

Rebecca laid a hand on Melody's arm. "I'm so sorry. Elizabeth and Julie are very protective of Hudson, especially Elizabeth. He says she's like a second mother."

"Maybe *you* don't believe I'm a gold digger, but it doesn't bode well for any relationship I might like to have with Hudson if two of his sisters do."

"They'll come around."

Melody stared at Rebecca. Was that really true? And who was Nicole? Should she ask? Opposing thoughts danced through her mind like the lights beaming off the glass enclosure surrounding her. She had to know. "Who's Nicole?"

"A woman who broke my brother's heart, pretending to love him when all she wanted was a rich husband."

"Oh." Melody had no idea what to say. "I'm not sure how I feel about Hudson."

"Think about giving him a chance. I promise you won't be sorry."

Melody wished she could be sure. Everything in her wanted to believe Rebecca, but she feared being reeled in only to be cut loose when she got too close. Was Hudson really waiting for her to make the first move, or would it be a replay of the mean girls' ploy that still haunted her so many years later?

Throughout the remainder of the evening, Melody studied the people around her. Elizabeth and Julie preserved their masks of friendliness, but Melody knew the thoughts behind their facades. She'd come to believe Hudson had been right about his father. H.P. did like her, but would that translate into approving of Hudson's interest in her? Likewise with Susan. Rebecca was the only one who was definitely in her corner.

As Hudson and Melody said their good-nights, she wondered whether she should act on his sister's urging to give him a chance. Since Christopher's death, she had wrapped her emotions in a cocoon, hoping to avoid more pain. But every time she interacted with Hudson, his kindness, sense of humor and dedication to The Village worked to unravel the protective barrier. Christopher would want her to be happy. He had always told her to reach for her dreams.

Did she have enough fortitude to tell Hudson that she wanted to go out with him again and find out what the future might hold? Would she finally be brave enough to put her fears behind her?

Chapter Ten

The headlights beamed into the darkness as Hudson drove down the blacktop road that led away from his parents' house. He turned on the radio to fill the silence. Melody had said few words since she'd gotten into the car. He didn't know whether to ask if something was wrong or keep quiet. After his conversation with Elizabeth, he feared she'd spoken with Melody, as well.

Anger at his sister stewed inside him until it was ready to bubble over. She had no evidence that Melody was after his money like Nicole, but nothing he'd said would convince his overbearing sister that Melody was the kindest, most generous and giving woman he'd ever known.

His anger cemented the notion that trying to convince his dad that Elizabeth should take over the company was a mistake. That meant he would become the company head. He'd been resisting the idea for years. Was he prepared to take on that task?

More than ever, he wanted to toss aside that stupid promise not to ask Melody for another date. But if he broke that promise, would she believe he could keep his word going forward? He was stuck between two rotten choices concerning Melody *and* his role with the company.

Why had he thought his presence alone would change Melody's mind about going out with him? Had he been too confident that he could win her over just by being around her?

"You're awfully quiet." Hudson looked her way as he pulled his car to a stop at a traffic light. Had someone—Elizabeth to be exact—said something unkind to Melody?

"I was remembering how much your dad enjoyed that game of Uno." Melody chuckled. "He was like a big kid."

"Don't let him fool you. It's his competitive nature that brings on his game face. He'll never let you see him sweat."

"Are you competitive, too?"

"It depends on the event." Competitive when trying to win Melody's favor. Or was that actually true? Had he used that promise as an excuse not to go after what he wanted because he feared she might turn out like Nicole? Elizabeth and her accusations about Melody had made him angry, but what could he do about it? Some of the same doubts plagued him.

"Uno must not be the kind of event that brings out your competitive nature."

Hudson shrugged as he pulled onto the highway. "We kind of let Dad win on his birthday."

"Does he know this?"

"Maybe, but it's all in good fun. And what he doesn't know won't hurt him."

"Are you sure?"

"It's just a game."

"What about stuff that isn't a game?"

Hudson frowned. "What are you getting at?"

"After meeting your family, I'm rethinking what I told

you about letting Elizabeth run your family company."
Melody paused, but took a deep breath and continued
before Hudson could respond. "I know you'd prefer to
be out on your own, but it wouldn't be right for you to
take control, then hand the company over to your sister.
It would be a deception."

"Great minds think alike."

"Are you saying you had the same thought?"

Hudson nodded. "As much as my dad grates on me,
I wouldn't want him to think I was betraying his trust."

Melody hung her head. "I'm sorry I even suggested it.
I feel terrible about it, but I wanted to help."

Hudson's heart thudded as he glanced at her down-
cast posture. He reached across the console and gently
squeezed her arm. "There's nothing to be sorry about.
Sometimes a certain path looks good until you take a
second look. I've taken several wrong turns in my life."

She looked up. "Thanks for being so kind in light of
my error in judgment."

"Honestly, you don't have anything to apologize for."
Hudson wanted so much to make her feel better, but he
was at a loss. When it came to Melody, he couldn't quite
get it right. As hard as he tried, he couldn't get that idi-
otic promise off his mind. He wanted to wish it away—
go back in time and undo it. But he was stuck with it.
He'd fallen into a trap of his own making.

Melody fell silent again as Hudson turned onto the
road that led to her subdivision. What was she thinking?
He was afraid to ask her what she thought of his family,
especially if Elizabeth had cornered Melody and warned
her away from him. If Elizabeth hadn't talked to Melody,
he would make things worse by mentioning it.

Hudson pulled into her driveway and turned off the

engine, but he made no move to get out of the car. Was there any chance she would invite him in and extend the evening? So much wishful thinking plowed through his brain that it made his head hurt and his heart ache.

"Thanks for sharing my dad's birthday. I liked having you there. It made the whole affair much brighter."

She shrugged. "I didn't do anything."

"You gave everyone things to think about, but your presence made everything better."

Melody stared at him in the dimly lit interior of the car. Licking her lips, she looked as though she wanted to say something, but uncertainty radiated from her eyes. "You're too kind. I guess I'd better go in."

"Sure. I'll walk you to the door." As Hudson jumped out of the car and raced around to open the car door for her, he wished he could come up with a reason to linger longer, but nothing came to mind. Maybe he should tell her he wasn't going to keep his promise and see what she said. It couldn't be any worse than waiting around for her to make a move.

When they reached her front porch, she already had her keys in her hand. Not a very promising sign for prolonging their time together. She unlocked the door and let it swing open as she turned back to him. He couldn't read her expression as she stood there silhouetted against the light she'd left on inside. His heart thundered, and he swallowed hard. How he'd love to kiss her right now.

"I…" They both spoke at once, then laughed.

"Ladies first."

She turned just enough for the light inside to expose the uncertainty still in her expression. "I'd like to talk to you about something if you have time."

"My time is yours."

"Good. Come in."

"Sure." Despite Melody's invitation, her voice projected that same doubt he'd seen in her eyes. What did she want to talk about that made her so tentative? Whatever it was, it must not be good. He followed her into the house and stood there in her front hall, a sick feeling in his gut.

She gave him a reluctant smile. "You're welcome to make yourself comfortable in the living room. I'll be back in a minute."

Her minute seemed like forever while he paced back and forth, his mind whirling with all kinds of trouble. Could something be wrong with his project? Surely not after she'd praised everything about it tonight. It couldn't be about the road rally. That was going well, too. The only thing left was his biggest fear. Elizabeth. Maybe he'd been right and his sister had confronted Melody, and she wanted to discuss it. That would explain her hesitancy about this meeting.

"Would you like something to drink?"

Hudson stopped pacing at her return. He wanted to get this conversation over with. "No, thanks. I've already had enough to eat and drink tonight."

"Okay. Me, too, actually." She let out a nervous little laugh as she scurried to the couch and sat down. "Please have a seat."

Hudson glanced around the room. He opted for the chair, so he could face her while he heard what she had to say. "What's this about?"

She took a deep breath and let it out slowly. She was killing him with this waiting.

"Don't be so nervous. Just tell me what's on your mind. I'm a big boy. I can handle whatever you've got to say."

Melody's worried expression morphed into a little smile. "I've changed my mind."

"About what?" A dozen thoughts zipped through his brain—none of them good.

She licked her lips again. "You said if I ever changed my mind about going out with you again to let you know. Well, I'm letting you know."

Hudson closed the gap between his chair and the couch in a nanosecond. He took her hands and pulled her to her feet. He couldn't help grinning from ear to ear. "That's the best news I've heard all day, all week, all year. There's only one thing I want to do. Kiss you."

She looked up at him as she put her arms around his neck. "I can't think of anything better."

With his heart pounding, Hudson leaned closer. Their lips met, and he wondered how he'd managed to wait this long for this moment. He wanted this relationship to work. She made his life brighter in so many ways, and he wanted to do the same for her.

When the kiss ended, he held her close and whispered in her ear, "You've made me a very happy man."

She stepped back and looked up at him. "Me, too. Happy, that is."

Hudson chuckled. "What made you change your mind?"

Melody's brown eyes widened as if he'd asked her a question she couldn't answer. Then she lowered her gaze. Elizabeth's accusation slithered back into his mind. No. Melody wasn't a gold digger. She was genuine and loving, but her reluctance to give him a reason made the doubts linger.

Finally, she glanced up and gave him a tentative smile. "I can't continue to deny the attraction between us, and getting to know you *and* your family made me realize that. So if you want another date, you've got one."

Hudson grinned. "Another date it is. What should we do?"

"Kirsten told me that you're taking a bunch of guys out to race cars, and the ladies are planning to watch."

Hudson leaned forward. "Did I hear you correctly?"

Nodding, Melody took a deep breath. "Yes."

Hudson didn't miss the determination in her voice. "And to what do I owe this huge about-face?"

"It's something you love. It's part of who you are, and if I want to be a part of your life, I'll learn to deal with it."

"Wow! So you've put your fears aside?"

She shook her head. "No, but I'm going to conquer them. I can't do that unless I face them head-on."

"I'm glad you're willing to do that." Her feelings had changed enough to go out with him again. He had to be grateful for that much now.

"I'm full of surprises."

"You certainly are, but we're not doing the car thing for a couple of more weeks. How about dinner and a movie this weekend?"

"Absolutely. That's more my speed anyway." She lifted her face to him.

He pulled her closer and kissed her again. She melted into his arms, and he never wanted to let her go. Finally, he held her at arm's length. She was everything he'd ever dreamed of in a woman, and he couldn't stop grinning. "Whatever we do, you can count on having the ride of your life."

The following Monday morning, Hudson awakened to a howling wind rattling at his bedroom window. He jumped out of bed, the wooden floor cold on his feet. He pulled aside the heavy drapery and looked out. A wall of white met his sight. Snow. The spring storm had hit with extra force. He hoped he could make it to The Village.

He got ready as quickly as he could, thankful when he was able to locate gloves, boots and a stocking cap—things he hadn't used in years. He donned his cold-weather gear and trudged through a foot of the white stuff. On his way to his SUV, he grabbed a snow shovel that was stuck in the corner of the garage and threw it into the back. He hoped he could make it to the main road without any difficulty, but the shovel could provide some insurance if the going got rough.

He managed to get to the main road, but the conditions were treacherous as the SUV swerved on the slick road-way. Although officials were telling people to stay off the roads, if at all possible, he had to get to The Village to make sure everything was okay with the construction site. The wind and blowing snow could pose a problem for the temporary coverings on the window openings.

Everything about the construction had been going well, except the workers at the factory had gone on strike, and only half of the new windows had arrived. They'd been waiting on the rest for several weeks, and when they'd finally arrived, he'd given the go-ahead to remove the old windows and put up temporary coverings. The plan had been to install the new ones today, but he hadn't planned on the storm being this bad. Now he wondered about the wisdom of that decision.

With great difficulty, Hudson managed to make it to The Village, but the main gate was closed because the electricity was out. As he stepped out of his SUV, Adam, along with some women he recognized as folks

who worked at the senior center and nursing home, ar-
rrived in a National Guard vehicle.

Adam waved as he approached. "I wasn't expecting
to see you here today."

"I was worried about what the storm might have done
to the building project."

"As you can see, we've lost power except in the senior
center and nursing home, where we have backup genera-
tors." Adam shook his head. "I can be thankful for that,
but the rest of the buildings could have problems if the
power's out too long."

"Yeah, it's not supposed to warm up much in the next
few days."

"Watch yourself when you get near the trees. Some
of those tall spindly pines can topple over because of the
weight of the ice and snow."

"I'll be on the lookout for them."

"After you make your inspection, we can meet in the
senior center. We might have a lot of people camping out
there if the electricity doesn't come back on."

"See you in a while." Hudson loped off across the
quad, leaving footprints as he went. He passed by the
fountain with its water flow stopped in a frozen mound. If
it wasn't for the worry clouding his mind, he might have
enjoyed the beauty of everything covered in pure white.

As he walked through the winter wonderland, he
pulled his phone from his pocket and called Melody. He
wanted to be sure she had power. When she answered the
phone, his heart did a little tap dance. "Hey, you okay?"

"I'm good other than I'm having to shovel my driveway and sidewalks. Why?"

"There are a lot of people without power. I wanted to
check on you."

"Thanks. That's sweet." He could hear the smile in her voice. "What about you? Are you okay?"

"I'm over here at The Village. I was worried about the construction site."

"You managed to get there from your place? How are the roads?"

"Not good." Hudson's stomach sank as he drew closer to the building. Several gaping holes where windows used to be greeted him. "And things are not looking so good here, either. A large pine tree has fallen and crashed into one of the temporary window coverings on the second floor."

"At least it only damaged a temporary covering and not one of the new windows."

"Leave it to you to look on the bright side." Hudson chuckled. "I've got to see what other damage the storm has caused. I'll call you later. Don't wear yourself out shoveling."

"You be careful, too, and stay warm."

"Okay."

Melody's words warmed him. "I'll try to stop by your place after I get done here. I…I'll talk to you later. Bye."

Hudson ended the call and stared at his phone. He'd almost told her how much he cared about her, but he'd stopped short. How did she feel about him? He knew she cared, but how much? He shook the questions away. He had to concentrate on the problems right in front of him. He looked at the tree sticking through the opening on the second floor and got a sick feeling in his gut. He didn't want to go inside. He imagined the worst, but he couldn't put off the inspection.

He punched in the code, thankful that the coded locks didn't require electricity. He pushed open the door and looked down the dark hallway. Even in the dim light, the dusting of snow on the concrete floor was visible. He swallowed hard. How much of it had blown into the building? He shivered against the cold and his fear of what he would find.

He entered the first apartment and saw that like the hallway, the floor was covered with a thin layer of snow. He soon moved on to the others and found them in much the same condition. He was ready to breathe a sigh of relief until he climbed the stairs to the second level. There he found coverings off half the windows. Snow filled the tubs and sinks while an inch or two covered the floors.

Rubbing a gloved hand down his face, he closed his eyes. He was in charge, and he had to find a way to minimize the damage. As he went back down the stairs, he shivered. The cold wind blowing through the structure went straight to his bones despite his warm clothes. Or maybe the thought of this predicament sent shivers down his spine. There was no time to feel sorry for himself. He had to take action, and that meant returning to his SUV for the shovel, so he could start removing the snow before it melted all over and created a bigger problem. No one would show up for work to help him today. He was on his own.

What would his father say if he saw this fiasco? As Hudson traipsed back across campus, dozens of what-ifs crowded his thoughts. Had he been distracted by Melody and their budding relationship and not considered the effects of the storm? Possibly, but the forecasters had predicted a couple of inches, not a foot of windblown snow. No matter the reason for what had happened, he had to take care of it.

After he returned with the shovel, he scooped up the

snow and threw what he could into the bathtubs or sinks. He would let it melt and go down the drain. As he finished clearing out the apartment at the far end of the hall, he thought he heard someone calling his name. But maybe the howling wind was playing tricks on him.

"Hudson, where are you?"

His heart took a leap as he finally recognized Melody's voice. He hadn't been hearing things. Shovel in hand, he stepped into the hallway. She stood just inside the door, but even in the dim light, he couldn't miss her in that red parka. He loved her in red. "Here I am. How'd you get here?"

"One of my neighbors has a four-wheel-drive vehicle, and he brought me over. I helped Adam get people settled in the senior center, and then I thought to see if you could use some help."

Laying his shovel aside, he closed the gap between them and gave her a hug. The cold fled. She warmed his heart and made everything about his life better, even this trouble. How was he going to keep from telling her how much he cared? He wished he could, but he had to give her time to see where their relationship would take them. And wasn't that what he should do, too, instead of throwing caution aside?

She grabbed her shovel and held it up. "I'm ready to go to work."

"I've finished scooping up the snow on this level. So you can help me upstairs." He walked with her to the second floor and went into the closest apartment. "Move the snow into a pile, then shovel it into the sink or bathtub, whichever is closest."

Melody pointed to one of the kerosene heaters they always kept around during the construction process. "Why don't you turn it on to warm up the place?"

"I thought I ought to get the snow out of here first and get the windows covered again before I wasted fuel warming the outdoors."

"That makes sense." Melody pushed her shovel along the floor, gathering snow as she went.

"I'm going to remove the tree in the next apartment and put plywood back on the windows." Hudson gave her a peck on the cheek. "We'll warm up in the senior center when we're done."

"Got it. I'm a lean, mean, snow-scooping machine."

Hudson chuckled as he walked out. "Don't work too hard."

Hudson took a look at the tree protruding through the window opening. He needed a chain saw but didn't have one on hand. He grabbed his phone and called Adam, explaining the situation. Minutes later someone from maintenance brought Hudson the handheld machine, and together they cut the tree out of the window, then cut up the rest of it into smaller pieces for easy removal.

Finally, Hudson replaced the plywood there and at the other windows. He braced them, praying that the temporary covering would stay in place this time. After he'd pounded the last nail, he poked his head into the room where Melody was working. "Looks as if you're about done."

She looked his way with a smile as she dumped a shovel full of snow into the kitchen sink. "That's the last of it. Should I turn on the water to melt it?"

"It should melt on its own after we fire up these heaters, but sure. You can turn it on until I get these started."

"Nothing's coming out." Melody turned the faucet to the off position and turned it on again.

Hudson shook his head. He didn't want to believe the

pipes were frozen, but there wasn't any other explanation. Just one more thing he didn't need. "I'll start the heaters, then turn off the main water supply."

Melody frowned. "Why?"

"Frozen lines often result in broken pipes. We'll have problems when the pipes thaw, but hopefully we can keep the damage to a minimum if we turn off the water."

Hudson fired up the heaters, then after finding the blueprints he rolled them out on the nearby kitchen counter. "Looks as if the main valve is at the back of the building. I hope it's not buried under too much snow."

He made his way around the building. The worst of the weather had subsided. Quiet surrounded him as he dug through the snow, searching for the valve. Thankfully, he discovered it without too much trouble. As Hudson started back around, Melody waved as she walked toward him. Before she reached him, a loud crack shattered the quiet, and Hudson looked up just in time to see a tall pine falling toward her.

"Melody!" Hudson yelled at the top of his lungs. With his heart nearly stopping, he ran faster than he'd ever run in his life. He reached her and tackled her as they both fell into the snow just a few feet away from where the pine landed with a resounding thud. Hudson held her tight as they lay together in the cold. What would he have done if something had happened to her?

"Are you okay?" His voice sounded shaky in his own ears.

She nodded but didn't say anything.

"Can you get up?"

"Yes." She let out a harsh breath as she extracted herself from his embrace and scrambled to her feet, dusting the snow off her coat.

Hudson popped up and did the same, the whole time thinking that he could've lost her. His heart still racing, he didn't want to let her out of his sight.

She launched herself at him and hugged him tight. "You saved me. Thank you."

He held her tighter. Everything in him wanted to spill out his feelings for her. He'd thought about it all day; the words were on the tip of his tongue. He had to fight not to say them. She'd just agreed to date him. He'd have to take it slow for both their sakes. Reluctantly, he released her. "Let's go get warm."

Hudson and Melody walked arm in arm to the senior center. The cafeteria bustled with young and old as folks from the women's shelter and children's homes found their way into the warmth. Adam waved for them to come over to his table, and they soon enjoyed lunch and visited with him and several of the residents, including Brady's grandmother Cora. Despite the cold and snow, a jovial mood prevailed, and Hudson tried not to think about his own problems.

After they ate and chatted for a little while, he stood. "I'm going back over to see if the heaters have warmed the building enough to thaw out the pipes."

Melody looked up at him. "Do you need my help?"

"No, you've already helped enough today. I'm sure you have things of your own to tend to. I'll give you a call when I'm finished."

She hopped up and gave him a hug before he left. "I'll be waiting."

Still feeling Melody's embrace, he jogged along the edge of the quad, the air cold even though the sun had chased most of the clouds away. He punched in the code and opened the door. The sound of running water greeted him. Frowning, he ran toward the sound.

He stopped short when he saw water pouring from a light fixture in the hallway. Where was that coming from? He'd turned off the water valve, or had he? He took the stairs two at a time and found water rolling out of the nearby doorway. Hudson stepped gingerly through the flood and discovered water pouring out of the sink where Melody had turned on the faucet.

Hudson ran over and turned it, but water still sprayed from the broken pipes underneath the sink. He wondered how many other apartments had broken pipes, but he didn't waste time looking. He raced back outside to the water valve. He got down on his knees and tried to figure out why the valve hadn't turned off the water. He grabbed the knob with both hands and gave it a twist. It moved another half turn. The cold had probably kept him from turning it off completely the first time.

He hurried back inside to see if the water had stopped. He splashed through the puddles and sprinted up the stairs. Nothing was coming out of the faucet. He sank against the wall and let out a harsh breath. He'd thought things were bad before. Now he had double the disaster to deal with.

Hoping against hope that he wouldn't find extensive losses, he traipsed through the building as he examined every apartment. Using his phone, he made a note of the broken pipes, falling ceilings and damaged wallboard. The list made him sick, but he couldn't wallow in self-pity. He'd asked for the job, and now he had to make the best of a bad situation.

He needed time to formulate a plan. He needed a quiet place to think. Without a second thought, Hudson headed for the chapel. He wouldn't find heat there, but maybe he would find peace and an answer for his troubles.

The snow sparkled in the waning sunlight as Melody made her way to the construction site. Hudson hadn't called, so she figured he must still be working. Warm air greeted her when she opened the door. That was a good sign, but the puddles standing everywhere were not.

She called Hudson's name. No response came. She called again, then ventured down the hallway looking in each door. There was no sign of him, but the scene before her made her stomach sink. What had happened since she'd been here earlier? She grabbed her phone and called Hudson.

When he answered, she could hear the sorrow and weariness in his voice.

"I'm here at the construction site. Where are you?"

"In the chapel."

"Do you want to be alone?"

"Not now. I could use your company if you don't mind the cold. It's not very warm in here."

"I'll be right over."

A few minutes later she found Hudson sitting on the front pew and sat beside him. He didn't say anything at first, just looked at her with sad eyes. Her heart was breaking for all his trouble. She sat there in the silence with him and prayed.

"Did you see the damage?"

His question caused her to look up. Melody nodded. "What happened?"

Hudson quickly explained.

Melody wrinkled her brow. "If I'd turned off that faucet, there wouldn't be all that damage."

"Not true." Hudson put an arm around her shoulders and drew her close. "The broken pipes still would've sprayed water everywhere. There might have been a little less water, but it wasn't your fault. I didn't get that valve off. The blame clearly lies with me."

"What are you going to do?"

Hudson took a deep breath. "Insurance will cover the cost of the new materials and repairs, but not the cost of hiring more workers. And I'll have to do that so we can finish the project on time."

"Time isn't that important. It'll get done when it gets done."

"It is to me and to my father. If I don't come in on time and under budget, he'll say he was right about the construction division. It's a money pit and should be sold or even shut down."

"But don't you have other projects that are doing fine?"

"Yeah, but this is the one that's under the most scrutiny."

"Why?"

"Because it's the one I insisted on undertaking when I took over the construction division. So this is the one that sits squarely on my shoulders."

"Have you ever thought that there might be a message in the fact that one thing after another has gone wrong? First Carter, then the stuff with the windows and now this. Maybe these things are trying to tell you to consider your father's request. Would that be so bad?"

A muscle worked in Hudson's jaw. "So you're on his side and not mine?"

Melody cringed at the accusation. "I'm on your side, but I'm asking you to think about it."

"I've considered it, and I've rejected it. End of story."

He was being as stubborn as his father. No wonder the two men butted heads. "Maybe it'll be the end of the story whether you like it or not."

"Not if I have anything to say about it. Conrick Construction has given work to a lot of veterans, and that's important to me. I want to make sure that continues." Hudson narrowed his gaze. "I'm not giving in no matter what problems arise."

Melody nodded. "I see your point. So what's your plan?"

"I'm not quite sure. I've been sitting here thinking and praying." He let out a loud sigh. "I inherited some property in South Georgia from my mom's parents, and I've had some inquiries from a company who wants to purchase some of the timberland. I can use that money to pay the new hires."

"Yes, your mom told me about that property."

"She did?"

"Yeah, the day that I had lunch with her ladies' group."

Hudson sat back in the pew and stared straight ahead. "Do you suppose she'd be upset if I sold part of it? That's why I never followed up on the inquiry before."

"I don't know." Melody took Hudson's hands in hers. "Let's pray about it together. Ask God to help you know about selling it. Getting the asking price without negotiation would be a sure sign."

"No doubt. That doesn't happen often."

While they prayed, she thought about how important Hudson had become in her life. He'd constructed a place in her heart that she couldn't easily tear down, and she was ready to find out how he fit into her life.

When they finished, he looked up. "I like having you to pray with and talk to."

"Didn't seem like that a few minutes ago."

Hudson gave her a wry smile. "I like it that you're not a yes-woman. You let me know what you think."

"I'll try to remind you of that when we disagree." Melody chuckled.

Hudson grabbed her hand and pulled her up from the pew. "Let's go get warm."

"Come over to my place. I have heat and electricity, and I can fix you dinner."

"Now, that's an offer I can't refuse."

"Do you need to go back to the construction site?"

Hudson shook his head. "There's nothing more anyone can do there tonight. Hopefully, people will be able to get to work tomorrow, and we can start putting things back together."

As they left the chapel, the sun had disappeared behind the trees surrounding the campus. Its disappearance brought with it even colder temperatures. Melody shivered and Hudson pulled her closer as they walked together. As they reached the front gate, the light inside the guardhouse flickered to life.

Melody glanced up at Hudson. "The electricity's back."

"Good news for everyone." He squeezed her shoulders. "Tomorrow's a new day and a new beginning."

"It will be." She waved as she opened her car door. "I'll see you at my house."

As Melody drove back home, she noticed the main roads had been cleared, but the side ones still had a snowy coating. She thought about her day with Hudson and how they'd been brought closer even in their disagreement. Was it safe to fall in love with this man? Would God guide her in this, too? She had to believe He would.

Chapter Eleven

The spring sunshine warmed Melody as she tried to put aside her worry. She sat in the stands with Annie, Kirsten and several other wives and girlfriends who'd come to watch Hudson and a number of the guys from The Village race around the track in their cars. The past two weeks had been some of the happiest times of her life, and she forced herself to think about the good things.

Every day she and Hudson shared lunch together at the senior center. She loved to listen to his enthusiastic talk about the progress of the women's shelter project. The damage wasn't as bad as it had first appeared, and he'd been able to hire new workers. The sale of the timberland was a done deal. God had given an affirmative answer to a lot of prayers.

Slipping out of her jacket, she wished this display of testosterone didn't make her so nervous. Even the sun couldn't warm her heart and take away the dread that sat there like a ball of ice. She'd made herself come to this thing because Hudson loved it, but every time a car swerved or a tire squealed, her heart was in her throat. Everyone else seemed to be enjoying it. Why couldn't she?

The bright sunshine glinted off the windshield and shiny red exterior of Hudson's Ferrari. Engines whined as the cars sped around the track. Melody's heart raced as Hudson left the other cars in the dust. Despite the speed, he'd explained that today was more about testing driving skills rather than a competition.

Melody glanced over at Annie and shouted above the noise, "It's so loud."

Nodding, Annie smiled, not trying to converse.

After the cars drove numerous laps, they stopped in one of the pit areas in the center of the track. Melody looked over at Annie again. "Do you know what they're doing now?"

"Ian said something about each driver doing a solo run for time."

"You mean like a race?"

"Not against each other. Against the clock."

"Well, it still sounds like a race to me."

Annie chuckled and patted Melody's arm. "Relax. They're having fun."

"But I'm not."

"I can tell." Annie laughed again.

Kirsten pointed to the death grip that Melody had on her purse strap. "Your knuckles look as white as mine did when Brady took me on that hot-air balloon ride."

Melody grimaced. "I'll be glad when they're finished."

Annie squeezed Melody's shoulders. "I'm so happy that you and Hudson are dating. I knew when I saw you two together at the fund-raiser that you were meant for each other."

"That remains to be seen."

Kirsten gave Melody a knowing glance. "I don't have any doubts."

Melody wasn't going to express hers, like the disapproval of Hudson's sisters. Today was about trying to cast her doubts aside, though they crowded into her thoughts as fast as the cars on the track.

When the racing was done, Hudson jogged across the track to where she was in the stands. Melody's heart soared. She was determined to put aside her trepidation to please this man who'd captured her heart.

When he reached her side, he gave her a peck on the cheek. "Did you enjoy your first race?"

"You don't want to know."

He gave her a quizzical smile. "Sure I do."

"Let's just say it was noisy."

"Looks as if you got a little sun today. I see a few freckles dotting that pretty nose of yours."

He leaned over and planted another quick kiss on the tip of her nose.

"It'll probably be pretty and pink tomorrow." Melody shook her head. "Even when I put on sunscreen this pale skin burns and those freckles pop out."

Hudson laughed and put an arm around her shoulders as they walked down the stands toward the track. "Let's head over to my place. I've got some of my famous barbecue sauce ready to pour over the pulled pork that's been slow cooking all day."

"You cook?"

"Only one of my many talents." Hudson chuckled. "Actually, the recipes belong to Sarah. She taught me everything I know."

"When you were growing up?"

"No, after I came back home and had to fend for myself. She gave me a crash course one weekend."

Hudson opened the door for her. Melody got inside

and buckled her seat belt. The familiar smell of leather combined with an almost sweet scent she couldn't define. "Is that the smell of your fuel?"

Hudson smiled at her. "Yeah. High-octane fuel. You like it?"

"Maybe."

"Then, maybe you've got racing in your blood. Would you like to take a trip around the track?"

Melody's pulse pounded. "Fast?"

"Yeah."

She could do this. If she did, she might understand why he loved this so much. "Okay, but don't laugh if I scream."

Shaking his head, he pressed his lips together, but he couldn't contain his laughter. "Sorry. I promise I won't laugh again, but your expression is priceless. You look as though you sucked on a lemon."

"I think I like lemons better than this." Melody narrowed her gaze. "How fast are we going to go?"

"How fast do you want to go?"

Melody took a deep breath. "I don't know. Don't tell me."

"You don't have to do this if you don't want to. It was only a suggestion."

Melody took another deep breath. "Let's do it before I change my mind."

"One trip around the track coming up."

Hudson revved the engine, and Melody's heart revved with it. In seconds they went around the first curve. They didn't seem to be going that fast, but maybe her mind was frozen with fear. She took a deep breath and tried to relax, but in the next instant she had no doubt the car was flying down the track, the engine putting out a high-pitched scream. She was about to scream along with it when the car suddenly slowed around the curve at the other end. Her eyes wide-open, she stared straight ahead as her pulse slowed along with the car.

Hudson brought it to a stop in front of the stands and grinned. "You want to know how fast we were going?"

Melody put a hand over her heart. "I need to recover before you tell me and send me into shock."

"Is it okay if I laugh now?" He burst out laughing.

"You laughed before I said it was okay."

"I couldn't help myself." He chuckled. "You didn't scream, but I wish someone could've taken a picture of your face."

Melody tried to frown at him, but a smile escaped instead. Did she really want to know how fast they'd been going? Since she endured the ride, she should know. "How fast?"

"On the straightaway—one hundred and seventy."

"Okay, that's faster than I ever want to go again."

"You know, you go much faster than that when you fly."

Melody flashed him an annoyed look. "I'm talking about in a car."

"I won't tease you again. You were a good sport, and I appreciate that more than you know. Now let's head to my place."

Melody nodded and settled back, happy and surprisingly relaxed. She'd never been to Hudson's home. He'd never said much about it. Where did the heir to a multimillion-dollar fortune live—in a luxury condo or a fancy house like his parents'?

As Hudson drove farther into the countryside, Melody

became more and more curious. "You really live way out here, don't you?"

"I do." He slowed the car near a large mailbox before turning onto a narrow blacktop drive lined with white fences and large bare-branched hardwoods. "This is it. My dad's grandparents used to own this property. They trained a few racehorses here, but after they quit, the old barns fell into disrepair and were torn down."

Melody couldn't believe her eyes as a white two-story structure with the massive wraparound porch came into view. The trees sheltering the house swayed in the wind. "It's beautiful. Hardly looks as if a bachelor would live here."

Hudson gave her a lopsided grin. "Are you saying a bachelor can't have a beautiful house?"

Melody shook her head. "I didn't mean it that way. It just looks like a family home, not a bachelor pad."

"It was a family home. My dad grew up here."

Hudson parked his car in one of the bays of the multicar detached garage behind the house. As they walked to the back door, Melody pulled her jacket up against the wind. "The temperature has really dropped. I hope we're not getting another snowstorm." She shook her head.

"No, just some colder weather. One snowstorm a year is all Atlanta can handle."

"That's for sure. I'm so thankful everything has worked out with the construction."

"No one's happier than me."

"Have your parents said anything to you about the sale of the timberland?"

"They haven't expressed their approval or disapproval, and I won't ask." Hudson shrugged. "I'm hoping it's a matter of it being my property to use as I please. The main thing is keeping the house. That's important to my mom."

"Is the house as big as this one?"

Hudson shook his head. "Hardly, but it's comfortable. I'll take you there sometime, and we could swing by and visit your mom."

Melody smiled and nodded, but she wasn't sure what Hudson would think of her humble beginnings. She should know by now that it wouldn't make a difference to him, but it could to his family if their relationship got really serious. But she didn't want to give him a hint that such a trip might not be to her liking. "Sure. We can do that sometime."

"How about the weekend after the road rally?"

"I'll check with my mom to see if she has any plans." She almost hoped that would be the case.

"I'm eager to meet her."

"She'll enjoy getting to know you, too." Melody wished she could be as enthusiastic about the get-together as Hudson was. She tried not to think about it as she looked at the large pond off to one side reflecting the sun sitting just above the treetops. She would concentrate on the beauty of this place. "It's so serene here."

"Almost too peaceful when you live by yourself." Hudson went up the steps to the back door, stepping aside to let her into the enclosed porch.

The doorbell sounded from the front of the house and Hudson moved to answer the door. Melody meandered through the rooms as she marveled at the fine craftsmanship in the old house. Its historic features were uncompromised by the modern renovations and conveniences in the kitchen. Hudson's home was a treasure, and so

was he. That was becoming more and more apparent
with each passing day.

Soon everyone who'd shared the day at the racetrack
had arrived. The women oohed and aahed over the decor
and antiques while the guys exclaimed over the collec-
tion of old decoys in the study. As everyone talked and
laughed around Melody, she thanked God for these people and their friendship. She thanked Him for bringing
Hudson into her life and prayed for wisdom about their
relationship.

After a grand tour of the house, they all pitched in to
set the dining room table and bring the food in from the
kitchen. After they were seated, Hudson gave thanks
for the food and the day's activities. Soon they filled
their plates as more laughter and conversation echoed
through the room.

She glanced over at Hudson, who was joking with
Brady, Ian and Travis. Hudson fit into her world. The
question was, did she fit into his? Despite the good things
between them, Melody couldn't forget his sisters' unkind
comments. They'd punched a hole in her confidence.
She'd gotten over one hurdle with Hudson today. She'd
faced the fear of his racing and came through unscathed.
She still didn't like the activity, but she understood better why he enjoyed it.

She had to learn to be happy with today and stop bor-
rowing trouble from tomorrow.

The main street of Melody's hometown had a May-
berry feel that gave Hudson a glimpse into her childhood.
He glanced at her across the console of his SUV while
they waited at the one traffic light. She seemed distracted
or worried. He wasn't sure which. Was she uneasy about

him meeting her family? He'd had the same concern the night of his father's birthday party. "Are you worried that your mother won't like me?"

She jerked her head in his direction as a little frown puckered her eyebrows. "No."

"Then, don't look so apprehensive."

"After seeing your place, I realize that my Southern roots are a little different than yours. Not that I didn't know that before." She gave him that forced smile.

"Do you think that matters?"

Melody shrugged. "I wanted to prepare you for a little downsizing. When your mom talked about your property, she mentioned a farm. I had no idea you own nearly a thousand acres even after you'd sold part of it."

"It was a farm, at least all of it that isn't timberland. The land came into my mother's family at the beginning of the twentieth century. Because of the mismanagement of the previous owners, my great-grandparents bought the property for pennies on the dollar. My mother's ancestors were farmers who worked hard every day of their lives. I'm the beneficiary of their hard work, and I don't want to squander their legacy. That's why I had to deliberate long and hard about selling any of it."

"I'm sure they would be proud of the way you've used the money from the sale. Lots of people are benefiting from your generosity." Warmth radiated from Melody's smile this time. "But I still say it's not like any farm I've ever known. It's like something you see in the movies about old Southern plantations with Spanish moss dripping from the trees."

"Yeah, it's a special place for me. I loved going there when I was a kid. We swam in the lake and went hiking in the woods. There was an adventure around every bend and over every hill. We would ride horses, and Granddaddy would take me out on his tractor for a special treat."

"Sounds like fun." Melody pointed ahead. "Turn right at the stop sign and go five blocks, then turn left onto Magnolia Street. On that street go three more blocks to Oak Lane, the street where I grew up."

While Hudson drove slowly through the residential neighborhood filled with modest clapboard houses in a variety of colors, he tried to imagine Melody as a little girl running up and down the street or riding her bike. Her childhood had probably been carefree, not orchestrated like his. That was why he'd loved the farm so much. It was his chance to be unencumbered. He loved being with Melody because with her he was able to be himself. Everything they did together reinforced that idea. His doubts had disintegrated.

The weeks since Melody had agreed to date him had been a whirlwind of activities that they'd shared. The road rally had been a resounding success. The following weekend he'd escorted her to Kirsten and Brady's wedding. Hudson wondered what it meant that he'd grabbed the garter, but Melody had made no attempt to get the bouquet that had been deliberately tossed in her direction.

Was he way ahead of himself when he thought of her in terms of marriage? He was finding it harder and harder to hide his feelings. What would she say if he told her that he loved her? Did she feel the same?

He'd tried not to think about that question but concentrate on the good times they'd shared and the good things happening at The Village as the construction project drew closer to completion. A week ago they'd joined with Kirsten and Brady to rejoice in their adoption of

Zach and Tyler, the two boys who'd been under Brady's foster care. Hudson wanted to celebrate everything with Melody, including the opening of the new women's shelter.

And he'd been thinking of adding a personal touch. Would she consider skydivers as part of the ceremony, or would she balk at the idea?

Questions of all sorts floated through his mind, but today he had to concentrate on one thing—getting to know Melody's family.

"The white house with the blue shutters is the place." He saw her take a deep breath and put on that less-than-genuine smile again. "You can park out front."

A flowering dogwood tree in the front yard still had a smattering of white blossoms. Tall pines and gnarly oaks shaded the house while a chain-link fence surrounded the yard. Hudson parked, then hurried around to open Melody's door. He wished he could take away her anxious expression as he opened the gate and escorted her up the front walk.

Before they reached the three steps going onto the porch, a woman with short dishwater-blond hair opened the screen door and stepped out. He was looking at an older version of Melody. The resemblance between mother and daughter was remarkable.

"You're here! I'm so happy y'all could come for a visit."

Melody hurried to greet her mother with a hug, then turned to him. "Mom, this is my friend Hudson Conrick."

Hudson nodded, trying not to let the friend reference annoy him. They were more than friends. Why didn't Melody want to acknowledge that? "I'm pleased to meet you, ma'am."

"Please call me Regina." She extended her hand.

Hudson shook it. "Thank you for inviting me, Regina. Melody tells me I'm in for a treat because you're serving your fabulous fried chicken."

"Well, I know it's Melody's favorite." A pleased smile brightened Regina's face as she ushered them into the house. "I hope you don't mind that I invited Will and Rob and their families. It's not every day your brothers get to see you."

"That's super." Melody looked over at Hudson, her brow wrinkled. "I hope you don't mind."

"Not at all." Happy to meet more of her family, Hudson took in the pine flooring and overstuffed sofa and chair and the decor that featured the same pale blue color as on the shutters outside. The house was plain but neat and clean.

"I was fixin' to set the table." Regina turned toward the kitchen. "Your brothers should be here shortly."

Melody immediately volunteered to help, and Hudson insisted on helping, too, even though both women protested that he was a guest.

"This is my first chance to use Ms. Lily's china and sterling." Regina opened a built-in china cabinet on the far side of the small dining room. "Your daddy always said such finery wasn't necessary, but I just like to come in here and look at it sometimes."

"Momma, it does look nice here. It'll look even better on the table."

Regina took out a stack of plates with gold trim and a rose pattern on the edges and handed them to Hudson. "Ms. Lily was my neighbor for years, and she gave me these nice things when she became very ill because she said her kids and grandkids wouldn't appreciate them.

She was such a dear. I hated to lose her. She was right. After she died, her kids sold everything."

Melody hugged her mother. "Momma, I'm so glad she gave you these lovely things."

Laughing, Regina gave her daughter another stack of dishes. "It's so wonderful to have you here. I wish you lived closer."

"I've tried to get you to move up to Atlanta."

Regina waved a hand at Melody. "I'd never survive in the city."

"Where I live it's still more country than city."

"That's what you think. There's too much traffic for me. Besides, I don't want to leave my friends."

As they finished setting the table, Regina asked Hudson about his work. He only mentioned what he did at The Village. He didn't know what Melody had told her mother, but he wasn't going to talk about Conrick Industries if he didn't have to. Today he wanted to be plain Hudson, not Hudson Paine Conrick, the Fourth, heir to millions.

As Regina went to the kitchen to start the chicken, she insisted they relax in the front room. He followed Melody and sat on the sofa with her. She still seemed uncomfortable as she crossed and uncrossed her legs and picked at invisible lint on her slacks. Before he could question her about it, two little girls, full of giggles, raced into the house.

They stopped short when they spied Hudson. "Are you Aunt Melody's beau?" the taller of the two asked.

He grinned but remembered how Melody had introduced him to her mother. "Maybe you should ask your aunt."

The little girls gathered around Melody. "Is he?"

"He's my friend."

"Ah. That's no good." The older girl frowned and turned back to Hudson. "Grammy says Aunt Melody should get married, and she needs a beau to do that. So could you be her beau?"

He had no clue how to respond. He needed to think fast. "What should I do to make her my girl?"

"You could kiss her." The smaller girl looked him over as if she was trying to figure out if he was worthy of her aunt.

As Hudson struggled to come up with a response, two men, one toting a baby in a carrier, two women and two young boys entered the house and rescued him from the inquiries of the little girls. Melody sprang up from the sofa and hugged them all and cooed over the baby dressed in pink—a girl, for sure. Then Melody turned to him. "Everyone, I'd like you to meet my friend Hudson Conrick."

Trying not to let Melody's introduction bug him again, he shook hands with everyone as they said their names and the kids' names. Now he knew how Melody probably felt that day at his parents' house when she'd been introduced to twice as many people. He tried repeating the names in his head. Will was married to Lauren, and their kids were Chloe, Ella and Micah. Rob, the younger brother, was married to Dana, and their kids were Robbie and Grace.

Wiping her hands on her apron, Regina joined the group and doted on her grandkids while they bounced around her like jumping jacks. Despite Melody's denial of a serious relationship with him, happiness grabbed hold of him.

While she helped her mother and sisters-in-law put

the food out on the kitchen counter, the men got their children settled and served them at the kitchen table, all except baby Grace, who had fallen asleep in the carrier. With everyone gathered, Will gave thanks for the food. Then the adults filled their plates and went into the dining room.

Mealtime was filled with jovial conversation and laughter. Hudson saw how this family bonded together. The tension that often accompanied his family get-togethers was absent here. He envied their camaraderie. Did Melody realize what a fantastic family she had?

When the meal was over, everyone pitched in to clear the table. Then the women finished the cleanup in the kitchen while the men took advantage of the remaining minutes of daylight to take the kids outside. The children played tag and hide-and-seek while Hudson joined Will and Rob on the front-porch rockers.

Will gave Hudson a pointed look. "You're H. P. Conrick's son, aren't you?"

Hudson stared back and wondered how Will had made the connection. "I am. Do you know my father?"

"I've never met him, but Rob and I have done some contract work for the food-processing division of Conrick Industries. We have our own trucking business."

Hudson nodded and wondered what shoe would drop next. "That's great."

Will eyed Hudson. "I'm going to be honest. I don't want to alienate you, but I have to look out for my sister. I hope you're not toying with her affections. Just because you have a lot of money doesn't mean you can cozy up to her, then toss her aside when she no longer fascinates you. She's had enough heartache in her life."

Hudson sat back in the rocker. *Wow!* How could he

respond to that? After his experience with Nicole, he'd developed a reputation as a love-'em-and-leave-'em kind of guy. Had that history now followed him to this tiny town? Surely not. But Ian had warned him in a similar way. Melody had a lot of protectors. "I care a lot about your sister. She's very important to me. I don't know why you think I don't have her best interests at heart."

Will tapped his steepled fingers against each other as he stared at Hudson. "Melody would be mortified if she knew I was telling you this, but I won't stand by and see her hurt or used."

Hudson shook his head. "What makes you think I'm out to hurt her?"

"Experience."

"Care to explain?" Had these guys run into one of his old girlfriends—women who'd probably only pretended to be hurt? All they'd ever wanted was to have the connections he provided or the money he could spend on them.

"Sure. This town's made up of mostly poor and middle-class families, but there are a few very wealthy families who own most of the businesses. When Melody was in high school, a small group of these rich girls befriended her. She hung around with them, and they hooked her up with one of the guys in their group—one of the most popular football players. He invited her to a party. I'd never seen her so excited. She thought she was 'walking in high cotton,' as they say around here."

"And this guy did something to hurt her?" Hudson's stomach churned at the thought.

"Not just the guy, but the whole group. They'd invited her there to make fun of her, laughing at her clothes, her hair or anything they could tease her about." Will leaned forward, his gaze boring into Hudson. "They tore her clothes, threw her in the pool and took her shoes, then left her to walk home."

Hudson's heart hurt for Melody. "Were those kids punished for what they did?"

Will let out a disgusted laugh. "Are you kidding me? Their daddies protected them from any kind of repercussions. There are two kinds of justice in this town. One for the rich and another for the poor."

Hudson thought back to his childhood. Had he ever been mean to someone because they were poor? Probably not, because his circle of acquaintances didn't include them. He'd lived in a bubble of wealth. His time in the army had changed that perspective, but still, he didn't know how it felt to be without or living paycheck to paycheck. No wonder Melody had told him when they'd first met that she didn't believe she fit into his world. How could he show her that she did? "I'm sorry Melody had to go through that, but I don't plan to hurt her."

"That's what you say."

"What do you want me to do? Quit dating her right now? Won't that do exactly what you're warning me of—hurt her?"

"I suppose it would." Will broke eye contact as he shrugged. "I've probably spoken out of turn, but I love my sister and don't want to see her unhappy."

I love her, too. The words filled his mind, but he didn't say them. Melody should hear them first. "You know there are no guarantees in any relationship, but I promise I'll do my best to make her happy." Hudson waited to speak further until Will looked up. "At this point, Melody's the more reluctant participant in our relationship. Now I understand a little better why."

With a skeptical expression still on his face, Will stared back at Hudson. "Good."

Hudson wondered if he should tell Melody how he felt, or would he be pushing their relationship beyond where she wanted it to go?

Chapter Twelve

As they neared her house, Melody wondered why Hudson had been so silent during the drive. After meeting her family, did he have second thoughts about their budding relationship? He'd appeared to enjoy himself and had even invited her brothers to go hunting on his property. Did she dare ask?

"Why so quiet tonight?"

"I've got a lot on my mind." He looked straight ahead. "We're waiting on the inspectors to give us a certificate of occupancy. I hope there are no problems that delay the approval."

"Do you think there could be?"

He shook his head. "You never know what inspectors will find. You think you've got everything in order, and they come up with some little thing that's not right."

"Could that interfere with the grand-opening celebration?"

"I don't think so. We have a little leeway to fix any problems. I just don't want there to be any." Hudson gave her a halfhearted smile. "I'm glad Adam's excited to have the skydivers as part of the celebration."

"He did seem pretty enthusiastic." Melody had not shared Adam's delight when Hudson had mentioned the subject, but she'd resigned herself to that part of the program because she wanted to make him happy. "Is that all that's bothering you?"

"Should there be something else?"

She shrugged. "I was a little worried that you might not like my family."

"What gave you that idea?"

"I don't know. I thought you might see them as poor country bumpkins compared to your sophisticated family."

"I can't believe you said that. What happened to the woman who doesn't care about people's wealth or lack of it?"

"I still don't care about it, but—"

"But you think I do?"

"No." Lowering her head, Melody pressed her fingers to her forehead as she let out a big sigh. "I was wrong to say that, but I've been on pins and needles all day, worrying about what you'd think. Forgive me?"

"We're almost to your house. When we get there, we've got some things to discuss."

"Okay." She didn't miss the anger simmering beneath the surface of Hudson's statement, and he'd never said he forgave her. Why had she opened her mouth? Her own insecurities had brought her to this point. Could she undo the mess she'd made?

When they arrived at her house, she hurried to unlock the door. Hudson remained silent as he followed her into the living room and sat on the couch. Her heart raced as she sat down beside him. Misery scrambled her thoughts as she stared at the picture on the opposite wall. Finally, she looked his way and read his unhappy expression. "All I can say is I'm sorry."

"I'm sorry, too."

Hudson's response clawed at her heart. She blinked hard to keep from crying. "I don't want you to be angry with me."

"I'm not angry. I'm hurt and disappointed."

"What can I say to make things better?"

He turned to her. "I don't know. You were worried from the beginning that we didn't fit into each other's worlds. I thought we'd gotten beyond that."

Melody tried to squash her heartache. "I want to tell you something, but I'm afraid it will make you even angrier."

"We might as well get everything out in the open. Let me have it."

"It has to do with Elizabeth and Julie." Melody swallowed hard.

Hudson frowned. "What about them?"

Melody took a deep breath, then told him what she'd overheard the night of his dad's birthday party. As she ended the story, she lowered her gaze. "So I let their words translate into worry about the way you'd look at my family. I know you better than that, so I have no excuse for what I said."

In a flash Hudson gathered her in his arms and held her tight. "Now I'm the one who's sorry. Elizabeth said much the same to me that night, but I had no idea you had accidentally heard her accusations, too."

Not expecting his reaction, Melody drank in the warmth of his embrace. "Thank you for understanding."

He held her at arm's length. "Seems we both have overprotective siblings."

Melody knit her eyebrows. "What do you mean?"

Hudson repeated the conversation he'd had with Will.

Melody covered her face with her hands. "How could he say those things to you? I'm so sorry."

"I'm sorry I didn't take your worry seriously after hearing Will's warning. I can see why that old incident coupled with my sisters' comments would make you question my thoughts."

"Can we have forgiveness all the way around?"

Gazing into her eyes, Hudson took her hands in his. "I only have this to say to you, Melody Hammond. I love you, and I don't want our families to come between us for any reason."

Had she heard him correctly? "Would you say that again?"

Hudson chuckled as he pulled her back into his arms. "Gladly. Melody, I love you."

Melody's heart soared. He loved her. "I love you, too. You've made me so happy."

"Me, too." Hudson settled back on the couch with an arm around her shoulders.

The day of the grand opening for the women's shelter had arrived. A wide red ribbon stretched across the entrance swayed in the gentle breeze. A jubilant crowd, including dignitaries and reporters, gathered nearby as they awaited the appearance of the skydivers who would open the festivities.

The noise of an approaching plane sounded overhead. Melody looked up as the four jumpers came into view, barely more than dots against the sky's blue canopy.

She shaded her eyes as the first parachute opened, its rainbow of colors brightening the sky. A second one opened, then the third as the skydivers maneuvered their parachutes in a zigzag pattern, following each other toward the earth. Melody waited for the fourth one, but the diver continued to plunge earthward, his chute not opening.

She let out a little cry as her heart sank to her stomach. She didn't want to believe her eyes. Did the rest of the crowd realize that there was a problem? She looked around, but it didn't seem as though anyone else was concerned. When she looked back up, the fourth diver's auxiliary chute opened—rounded and white compared to the colorful elliptical-shaped parachutes of the others.

With her heart still in her throat, Melody watched the first three divers make a pinpoint landing on the quad near the crowd. Loud cheers went up each time one landed. The odd parachute disappeared behind a stand of trees on the other side of the campus.

As the divers removed their helmets and gear, she could see that Hudson was missing. Melody wanted to scream as her stomach churned. How could she go through with the ribbon cutting without knowing he was okay?

Melody searched for Adam in the crowd. When she saw him approaching, she raced to his side. "Did you see?"

Adam nodded. "Looks as if Hudson's main chute didn't open. I've sent Jeremy to see where he landed."

"You sent a golf cart?" she asked in a harsh whisper.

"Take it easy. Jeremy can take the golf cart into places where a car can't go. Hudson will be okay. His auxiliary chute opened. He's an experienced skydiver. No need to worry." Adam patted her arm. "We've got to go on with the ribbon cutting."

Melody went through the ceremony like an automaton, her mind totally consumed with worry. Why was she the only one concerned about his safety? She kept looking over her shoulder hoping to see him, but the ceremony ended and still there was no sign of him.

After Adam announced the reception in the senior center dining hall, the crowd dispersed and Melody cornered Adam. "I'm going to find Hudson."

"No need. Jeremy called, and he's fine. He landed on the soccer fields in the adjacent park." Adam patted Melody's arm again. "I know you were worried, but Hudson told me this kind of thing happens in about one out of every thousand jumps. That's why they have backup chutes."

"You're right, but that doesn't make it any less frightening." Melody had no idea what she was going to say to Hudson when she saw him. She wasn't even sure she could talk to him without bursting into tears. She had to pull herself together before he arrived.

After Hudson joined the activities, she found no opportunity to talk privately with him. She managed to get through the tour of the facility and the reception while he hovered by her side. She smiled, but inside she was frowning. She thought she was okay with Hudson's risk-taking activities, but today's incident showed her that she wasn't. She couldn't feign acceptance of these pursuits.

When the festivities finally ended and Melody stood alone with Hudson in the hallway of the women's shelter, she hoped she could talk with him without crying. The smell of new construction permeated the air, but there was nothing new about her fears and the conversation she was about to have.

"That went well." He put an arm around her shoulders as he smiled down at her.

"Everything except you." Melody slipped out of his embrace.

"Well, other than that little incident." He gave her a lopsided grin as he held his arms up by his sides as if nothing had really happened. "I'm all in one piece. No problem."

"No problem?" She forced herself not to raise her voice. "It's a problem for me. I can't deal with it. I should've gone with my first instincts and never gotten involved with you, but I let you convince me that love conquers all."

"It can if you let it." His expression sobered.

"No, it can't." Melody took a deep breath. "I think it would be better for both of us if we stopped seeing each other. The construction is done. We can cut our ties since we no longer have to work together."

Hudson shook his head, disbelief in his eyes. "Melody, please reconsider. I won't skydive anymore. I won't race cars. I love you more than those things."

"No, Hudson, you can't give up your passions for me. You would come to resent me. There's no way we can find a compromise. Please accept this reality."

"I don't want to accept your reality."

"That's the way it is." Melody held up a hand. "I'm sorry. I'm leaving now. Please don't follow me."

Melody forced herself not to run or look back as she left the building. Once outside, she sprinted to her car while tears streamed down her face. Why couldn't love be simple? Why couldn't life be simple? *God, why did You let me fall in love with a man who likes to take chances?*

Sitting in her car, she gripped the steering wheel. She

squeezed her eyes shut and stifled the tears. She couldn't blame God, and she wouldn't cry. This was her own doing. She was the one who had ignored those doubts niggling at the back of her mind. Breaking up with Hudson was like pulling off a bandage—painful now, but the healing would come.

Two weeks later, Hudson's heart still ached. Melody's rejection had hurt more than he'd ever thought possible. Lovesickness—a perfect diagnosis. He'd wanted to argue with her that day, but he was wise enough to know that he would've been wasting his breath. This strong-willed woman didn't easily change her mind about anything, but why couldn't she see that he would give it all up for her?

Still, a twinge of doubt wouldn't let him go. Was she right? Would he come to resent her? Was God trying to tell him that they didn't belong together? He couldn't stop asking that question, but he never came up with an answer. Now his father had commanded him to appear. What other bad news was going to drop in his lap?

Hudson walked into his father's study. H.P. looked up from where he sat at his desk as Hudson stood there wondering what had prompted this meeting. The breakup with Melody had done nothing to improve his mood, and on top of that, he dreaded this conversation.

"Have a seat, son." H.P. steepled his hands and stared at Hudson. "I hope you're receptive to what I've got to say."

"I'll listen." He sat on the edge of the chair, not wanting to get too comfortable.

"Good. I know it hasn't been quite six months since you took over the construction division, but I don't want to wait to talk over what I'd like to see happen there."

Hudson wished he could walk out and never look back. But he loved his family and didn't want to alienate any of them, even his overbearing father. "Is this some kind of ultimatum?"

"Depends." H.P. leaned forward, a no-nonsense look in his eyes. "I've decided to retire. I've seen what you've done with the construction division, and I approve. You've demonstrated you're a good manager and leader. When trouble arose, you developed a plan to get through it, and you were successful. Your achievement there makes me even more certain you should take the reins of Conrick Industries."

Hudson drank in his father's praise—a rarity in his life, but even the longed-for approval didn't make him happy. He still didn't want to run Conrick Industries, but was there any point in arguing? It would probably be about as successful as arguing with Melody. "So what's your plan?"

"I'm glad you're willing to listen." A surprised smile curved H.P.'s mouth. "I'd like to retire by the end of the year. In the preceding months, I want you to work side by side with me. Then when I hand it over to you, I'd like you to bring Elizabeth on board. You were right. She has the qualifications and a lot of good business sense, just not the experience. You can teach her the ropes. After that the two of you can figure out whatever you'd like as to who's in charge going forward."

Hudson let his father's plan roll through his mind. His dad had actually listened to him and was willing to give Elizabeth a chance. "Have you talked to Elizabeth?"

"I haven't, because I wanted to run this by you first. I didn't want to do anything that didn't meet your approval."

At his father's statement, Hudson nearly fell out of his chair. "My approval?"

H.P. nodded. "I figured if I wanted your cooperation, I'd have to do a little compromising. What do you say?"

"I'd like to discuss it with Elizabeth." Hudson was still trying to grasp the fact that his father had changed his mind. He was giving Hudson what he wanted without another argument. Only Melody's change of heart would make this day better.

"You'll get your chance." His dad glanced at his watch. "She'll be here in a few minutes. And I've come to another decision. I plan to get rid of the construction division."

"How can you do that to Carter right after he's just gone back to work?"

H.P. held up one hand. "Hold on. Don't jump to conclusions. I think you'll like my idea."

As Hudson was ready to say something, Elizabeth walked into the room. She greeted them with a hug, then sat. "So what's the big meeting about?"

While H.P. explained his plan to Elizabeth, Hudson watched for her reaction. Would she be on board or critical? Would she be willing to share duties and take instruction from him? Ever since his conversation with her about Melody, Hudson saw his sister through a less-favorable lens. Seeing her reminded him of Melody's brother and his warning. He tamped down his anger while Elizabeth and H.P. discussed the plan. He wasn't going to have a relationship with Melody, so there wasn't any point in being upset with his sister.

"What do you think, Hudson? Are you willing to take me under your wing and teach me everything you know?"

He stared at her. Either she was very eager to get her

chance at running the company, or she was actually the older sister he'd always respected and admired, not the critical one he'd encountered a few weeks ago. "Are you willing to listen and work with me without criticism?"

She gave him a crooked smile. "Are you saying I can be argumentative?"

H.P. cleared his throat. "One more thing before I go. I'm handing the construction division over to Carter. It's his with the stipulation that he continue your policy of hiring vets. On that note, I'll leave you two alone to hash this out."

"Wait." Hudson jumped up. "What do you mean?"

"I mean I'm giving it to Carter—the whole thing." H.P. waved a hand in the air. "It's out of my hair, and it's going to someone who has earned it."

"Wow! Carter never said anything to me."

"I asked him not to until we drew up the papers. I hope you aren't disappointed."

"How can I be? You've made some excellent moves, and I can't argue. Thanks." Hudson shook his dad's hand, then hugged him as he realized his father may have orchestrated a few people's lives in his usual manner, but the wisdom of his decisions wasn't lost on Hudson. As H.P. left the room, Hudson looked at his sister. "Do you want to do this?"

Elizabeth nodded. "If you do, I'm in."

He extended his hand, forgiveness filling his heart. "Okay, partner."

"I'm glad we can work together." Elizabeth shook his hand, then let out a heavy sigh. "Rebecca told me that Melody broke up with you. I'm sorry."

"I thought that's what you wanted."

"I was wrong. I misjudged her." Elizabeth hung her

head. "If you change your mind about working with me, I'd understand. I'm so sorry. Please forgive me."

"I will only because your unkind words had nothing to do with our breakup. What you said wounded Melody, but that's not the reason we're not together anymore."

Hudson went on to explain the history between Melody and him. Rehashing their disagreement only produced a helpless feeling. He didn't know how to change Melody's mind. Their relationship had been doomed from the start. She'd recognized it, but he hadn't wanted to accept it. His whole life had taken a one-eighty. He had accepted the compromise with his father to run Conrick Industries and eventually hand the reins to Elizabeth. Hudson couldn't forget that the idea had originally come from Melody, but she wouldn't be around to see it come to pass.

Elizabeth sighed. "I'd like to help you work things out with Melody."

"Haven't you interfered enough already?" Hudson smiled wryly.

His sister shrugged. "I suppose, but I'd like to make amends."

He shook his head. "If you want to apologize to her, that's your business. I love you, big sis, but don't try to fix things for me."

"No promises."

Hudson took a deep breath. What would it take to change Melody's mind? Could he plead his case one more time to make her see that love could conquer all?

Life went on without Hudson. Melody filled her days with welcoming the new residents of the women's shelter, but every time she walked into that building her heart ached. She remembered how they'd worked together through the storm, how he'd saved her from the falling tree and how he'd kissed her. The memories plagued her, and she missed him so much that she was tempted to call him up and tell him she'd been wrong. But then she'd remember how his parachute hadn't opened and how her heart had flown into her throat and she'd died a thousand deaths until she knew he was okay. She couldn't live like that, and she'd be crazy to love a man who lived so dangerously.

Melody hurried down the hallway to the end apartment, where her new residents were gathered for their weekly Bible study. They studied the stories of deliverance in the Book of Daniel. And after their prayers, they ate and enjoyed each other's company. She thanked God that these women focused her mind on something else besides her heartache.

When the study was over, Hannah, one of the younger women, came up to Melody. "Thanks for leading that study. I appreciate all you've taught me since I've been here. I know I have a long way to go, but I'm learning to trust God to see me through my troubles. I have this verse on my mirror, so I look at it every morning when I get up."

"What verse?"

"Isaiah 26:3. 'You will keep in perfect peace those whose minds are steadfast, because they trust in You.' Trusting God takes away the worry. I wanted to let you know how much you've helped me do that."

"You're welcome, Hannah. I'm so glad." Melody gave the young woman a hug. "If you ever need me for anything, just call. Good night."

Hurrying across the quad toward the parking lot, Melody couldn't get Hannah's words out of her mind. *Trust-*

ing God takes away the worry. Melody had been telling others to have faith in Him, but she'd failed to do the same. She'd been living most of her life in fear and not relying on God. What kind of hypocrite was she?

She'd let worry ruin a loving relationship with Hudson.

As she got into the car, she let out the tears she'd been holding back for weeks. After she had a good cry, she wiped her eyes and nose, then prayed for strength to put her life and all her decisions in God's hands.

Despite her prayer, Melody wondered whether she could make amends with Hudson. Would he even want to talk to her after the way she'd shut him out? She had to believe that God would lead her in the right direction. She had to be patient enough to wait on His answer.

As those thoughts rolled through her mind, her phone rang. She grabbed it from her purse and looked at the screen. She gasped as she viewed the name. Elizabeth, Hudson's sister. What could she possibly want? Melody accepted the call and hoped for the best.

"Hello."

"Hi. I'm glad you answered."

"No problem. Why did you call?"

"First, I want to apologize for the things I said about you. Rebecca told me that you overheard my comments. I was wrong, and I'm asking you to forgive me."

Melody knew she should, but right now saying so would be a lie. "Is it all right if I tell you I'll work on the forgiveness?"

"Thanks. That's enough for now. I appreciate your honesty." Melody could hear the relief in Elizabeth's voice.

"That's one thing I know Hudson loves about you," Elizabeth continued. "You have to know, he really does love you, and he'd give up all those things you hate because he does. Besides, soon he'll be too busy to race cars and skydive. Our dad's retiring, and Hudson has agreed to take over the company."

"But that's the last thing he wanted to do." Melody couldn't believe it.

"They've come to a compromise. Hudson will take over the company, teach me the ropes, then turn the company over to me. Everyone wins."

"I'm glad y'all worked it out," Melody said. Could things work out for her, too? She'd finally discovered the key to riding out bumpy times. Trust in God. So simple, but she hadn't been doing it. She'd let fear rule instead of God.

"Will you give Hudson another chance?" Elizabeth said, interrupting her thoughts.

Melody's heart raced. "I was wondering whether he'd be willing to give *me* another chance. After all, I was the one who ended the relationship."

"There's a second chance for both of you. I want my little brother to be happy, and your presence in his life will do that."

"I hope you're right." Melody wondered how she could make amends with Hudson. Would he believe she was willing to accept him and everything he liked to do? She was determined to turn her worries over to God, even the fear of losing Hudson forever. She'd put her future in God's hands.

The warm day and the cloudless sky beckoned even the most timid skydiver, and that skydiver was Melody. This was the final frontier for conquering her fears. Her stomach roiled and her heart raced as she thought about jumping out of a plane at fourteen thousand feet. But she would do this to show Hudson once and for all that she loved him and could accept whatever he wanted to do in life.

The day after Melody's talk with Elizabeth, she had called and made the appointment for a tandem jump and requested Hudson as her instructor. When she walked into the skydiving center, folks of every age were getting ready. There was an older woman who was celebrating her sixty-fifth birthday, an eighteen-year-old girl out for a thrill and a middle-aged couple and their two adult children on vacation. If they could do it, so could she. She took a deep breath as she put on her red jumpsuit.

As she finished zipping it up, Hudson walked into the room with his pack. When he saw her, his eyes widened. "Why—"

"Why am I here?"

"Yeah."

"I'm doing a tandem jump with you."

He shook his head. "Why?"

Melody laughed. "Is that all you can say?"

"I can't believe you're here, and that you intend to skydive, and you still haven't told me why."

"I don't want your love of skydiving or anything else to stand between us." Melody stared up at him. "I'm sorry my fears got in the way of our love. I love you."

"Those are the best three words I've heard in weeks. But this?" Hudson held out a hand. "You don't have to prove anything to me. Your love is enough."

"But I have to prove it to myself. I've been living with fear, and I can't continue that way."

"Lots of brave people haven't jumped out of planes."

Melody smiled to stifle her nerves. "I know, but let me do this."

"Okay. I promise you'll be in great hands."

Melody stood on her tiptoes and kissed his cheek. "I know."

Saying a multitude of silent prayers, Melody listened to Hudson's instructions and explanation about what to expect. She absorbed the mental checklist. She prayed that her mind wouldn't blank and forget everything. She followed Hudson to the plane, a videographer recording this momentous occasion. As the plane took off and ascended, nervous laughter and joking filled the area. Hudson sat behind her, adjusting the harness that hooked them together. His talk was encouraging, and she loved the image of them tethered together on this adventure and in life.

When their turn came, he whispered in her ear. "You don't have to do this if you don't want to, but you can trust me to make this one of the best experiences of your life."

Trust. That one word spelled out the reason for this adventure. Melody took a deep breath, her stomach churning and her heart racing faster than the propellers on the plane. "I'm ready. Let's do this."

"Okay, brave girl, here we go."

They stood in the open door of the plane, and the next second they were falling through the air. She had done it. They had done it. They twirled and floated. It was like nothing she'd anticipated. The view was fantastic, but her heart, nerves and stomach were on overload. The jump was frightening and fabulous all at the same time. Her stomach had that elevator moment when the regular chute opened. Then Hudson instructed her on how to maneuver it. As they came closer to the ground, he took over and brought them in for a perfect landing.

Hudson was all smiles as he unhooked them and gathered in the chute. "What'd you think?"

Her legs shook as she managed a smile. "That was amazing. It's also the scariest thing I've ever done, and I don't ever want to do it again."

Laughing, Hudson held her close. "You're the amazing one. I can't believe you did that for me."

"Does this mean everything's good with us?"

"Better than good." He pulled her into his arms and kissed her.

A smattering of applause brought them out of their world for two. Hudson glanced at the people surrounding them. "Folks, I don't normally kiss my tandem partners, but this little lady and I have some future plans to discuss."

Arm in arm, they walked back to the building. Melody felt as if she was still falling through the air. She'd met her fears head-on. She had to remember that God was with her no matter what life brought her. Right now having Hudson in her life was better than she'd ever hoped for. She looked up at him. "So what about those future plans?"

"Are you willing to jump into this thing called love and see where it takes us?"

"Yes. I love you. If you race or skydive, I want to be there."

"I love you, too, and with you by my side, life will be better than ever." Hudson kissed her again.

"I'm ready for this big adventure with you." Standing in the circle of Hudson's arms, Melody gazed up at him, prepared to trust her heart to this man she loved.

* * * * *

Dear Reader,

Thanks so much for choosing to read *Falling for the Millionaire*, the third book in my Village of Hope series. I hope you enjoyed Melody's story. The Village of Hope is all about second chances. Melody and Hudson get their second chances at love, and she learns a special lesson about trusting God. It is important to remember that God's perfect love can take away our fears if we only trust Him.

I enjoy hearing from readers. You can contact me through my website, merrilleewhren.com, or through my Facebook page, facebook.com/MerrilleeWhren.Author. You can also write to me through the Harlequin Reader Service, PO Box 9049, Buffalo, NY 14269-9049.

May God bless you,

Merrillee Whren

COMING NEXT MONTH FROM
Love Inspired®

Available April 19, 2016

AN AMISH MATCH
Amish Hearts • by Jo Ann Brown

A marriage of convenience for widowed single parents Joshua Stoltzfus and Rebekah Burkholder will mean a stable home for their children. Becoming a family could also lead to healing their past hurts—and a second chance at love.

THE COWBOY'S TWINS
Cowboy Country • by Deb Kastner

Jax McKenna is exactly the man Faith Dugan needs to help her repair her horse sanctuary. But she never expects to fall for the hunky cowboy—or that he'll need *her* help raising the twins he finds on his doorstep!

CLAIMING THE SINGLE MOM'S HEART
Hearts of Hunter Ridge • by Glynna Kaye

Single mom Sunshine Carston is trying to gain a seat on the town council—against Grady Hunter's mother. So when Grady steps in to help when his mother falls ill, Sunshine is torn between winning...and wishing for a future with the rugged outdoorsman.

HER FIREFIGHTER HERO
Men of Wildfire • by Leigh Bale

Widow Megan Rocklin just wants to run her diner and keep her children—and her heart—safe from getting close to another man with a dangerous job. Catering meals for the wildfire hotshot crew was never part of her plan—nor was falling for their handsome boss.

COAST GUARD SWEETHEART • by Lisa Carter

Coast guard officer Sawyer Kole is back in town to fix his greatest mistake: abandoning the only woman he's ever cared for. In the aftermath of a hurricane, he'll help Honey Duer rebuild her lodge, but can he restore her faith—and love—in him?

HER TEXAS FAMILY • by Jill Lynn

Widower Graham Redmond is a single father focused on raising his daughter. But when free spirit Lucy Grayson starts working in his medical office, can he put aside his well-laid plans and see that she's the missing piece to make his family complete?

REQUEST YOUR FREE BOOKS!

2 FREE INSPIRATIONAL NOVELS
PLUS 2
FREE
MYSTERY GIFTS

Love Inspired®

YES! Please send me 2 FREE Love Inspired® novels and my 2 FREE mystery gifts (gifts are worth about $10). After receiving them, if I don't wish to receive any more books, I can return the shipping statement marked "cancel." If I don't cancel, I will receive 6 brand-new novels every month and be billed just $4.99 per book in the U.S. or $5.49 per book in Canada. That's a saving of at least 17% off the cover price. It's quite a bargain! Shipping and handling is just 50¢ per book in the U.S. and 75¢ per book in Canada.* I understand that accepting the 2 free books and gifts places me under no obligation to buy anything. I can always return a shipment and cancel at any time. Even if I never buy another book, the two free books and gifts are mine to keep forever.

105/305 IDN GH5P

Name	(PLEASE PRINT)
Address	Apt. #
City	State/Prov.	Zip/Postal Code

Signature (if under 18, a parent or guardian must sign)

Mail to the **Reader Service**:
IN U.S.A.: P.O. Box 1867, Buffalo, NY 14240-1867
IN CANADA: P.O. Box 609, Fort Erie, Ontario L2A 5X3

**Are you a subscriber to Love Inspired® books
and want to receive the larger-print edition?
Call 1-800-873-8635 or visit www.ReaderService.com.**

* Terms and prices subject to change without notice. Prices do not include applicable taxes. Sales tax applicable in N.Y. Canadian residents will be charged applicable taxes. Offer not valid in Quebec. This offer is limited to one order per household. Not valid for current subscribers to Love Inspired books. All orders subject to credit approval. Credit or debit balances in a customer's account(s) may be offset by any other outstanding balance owed by or to the customer. Please allow 4 to 6 weeks for delivery. Offer available while quantities last.

Your Privacy—The Reader Service is committed to protecting your privacy. Our Privacy Policy is available online at www.ReaderService.com or upon request from the Reader Service.

We make a portion of our mailing list available to reputable third parties that offer products we believe may interest you. If you prefer that we not exchange your name with third parties, or if you wish to clarify or modify your communication preferences, please visit us at www.ReaderService.com/consumerschoice or write to us at Reader Service Preference Service, P.O. Box 9062, Buffalo, NY 14240-9062. Include your complete name and address.

LI15

SPECIAL EXCERPT FROM

Love Inspired

A marriage of convenience for widowed single parents Joshua Stoltzfus and Rebekah Burkholder will mean a stable home for their children. Becoming a family could also lead to healing their past hurts—and a second chance at love.

Read on for a sneak preview of
AN AMISH MATCH by Jo Ann Brown,
available May 2016 from Love Inspired!

"Will you give me an answer, Rebekah? Will you marry me?"

"But why? I don't love you." Her cheeks turned to fire as she hurried to add, "That sounded awful. I'm sorry. The truth is you've always been a *gut* friend, Joshua, which is why I feel I can be blunt."

"If we can't speak honestly now, I can't imagine when we could."

"Then I will honestly say I don't understand why you'd ask me to m-m-marry you." She hated how she stumbled over the simple word.

No, it wasn't simple. There was nothing simple about Joshua Stoltzfus appearing at her door to ask her to become his wife.

"Because we could help each other. Isn't that what a husband and wife are? Helpmeets?" He cleared his throat. "I would rather marry a woman I know and respect as a friend. We've both married once for love, and we've both lost the ones we love. Is it wrong to be more practical this time?"

Every inch of her wanted to shout, *"Ja!"* But his words made sense.

She had married Lloyd because she'd been infatuated with him and the idea of being his wife, so much so that she had convinced herself while they were courting to ignore how rough and demanding he had been with her when she'd caught the odor of beer on his breath. She'd accepted his excuses and his reassurances it wouldn't happen again…even when it had. She'd been blinded by love. How much better would it be to marry with her eyes wide-open? No surprises, and a husband whom she counted among her friends.

She'd be a fool not to agree immediately. "All right," she said. "I will marry you."

"Really?" He appeared shocked, as if he hadn't thought she'd agree quickly.

"Ja." She didn't add anything more, because there wasn't anything more to say. They would be wed, for better or for worse. And she was sure the worse couldn't be as bad as her marriage to Lloyd.

Don't miss
AN AMISH MATCH
by Jo Ann Brown,
available May 2016 wherever
Love Inspired® books and ebooks are sold.

www.LoveInspired.com

"The name is Will Canfield," he said. "Thank you for your assistance, Miss Stone."

"You sure picked a dangerous place to take your baby for a walk, Daddy Canfield. Might want to reconsider your route next time."

The measured expression on his face faltered a notch. "Oh, this isn't my baby."

She hoisted an eyebrow. "Reckon who that baby belongs to is none of my business one way or the other." She gestured toward the child. "I think your girl is getting hungry. Better get mama."

"That's the whole problem." The man spoke more to the infant in his arms than to her. "Someone abandoned her. I found her on my doorstep just now." He glanced over his shoulder and then back at her. "The woman—the one who spooked the cattle. Did you see which way she ran? I think this child belongs to her. If not, then she might have seen something. She was hiding in the shadows when I discovered this little bundle."

"Sorry. I was focused on the cattle."

Clearly frustrated by her answers, Daddy Canfield muttered something unintelligible.

He grimaced and held the bundle away from him, revealing a dark, wet patch on his expensive suit coat.

Tomasina chuckled. The boys were going to love hearing about this one. They'd never believe her but they'd love the telling. Her pa always liked a good yarn, as well. At the thought of her pa, her smile faded. He'd died on the trail a few weeks back and they'd buried him in Oklahoma Territory. The wound of his loss was still raw and she shied away from her memories of him.

"Fellow…" Tomasina said. "As much fun as this has been, I'd best be getting on."

"Thanks for your help back there," Will replied, his tone grudging. "Your quick action averted a disaster."

The admission had obviously cost him. He struck her as a prideful man, and prideful men sometimes needed a reminder of their place in the grand scheme of things.

"Daddy Canfield," she declared. "Since you don't like guns, how do you feel about rodeo shows? You know, trick riding and fancy target shooting?"

"Not in my town. Too dangerous."

"Excellent," Tomasina replied with a hearty grin.

Yep. She felt better already.

Don't miss SPECIAL DELIVERY BABY
by Sherri Shackelford,
available May 2016 wherever
Love Inspired® Historical books and ebooks are sold.
www.LoveInspired.com